THE PROMISED HAND

Susan Wolfe

Writers Club Press

San Jose New York Lincoln Shanghai

The Promised Hand

Writers Club Press
an imprint of iUniverse.com, Inc.

For information address:
iUniverse.com, Inc.
5220 S 16th, Ste. 200
Lincoln, NE 68512
www.iuniverse.com

ISBN: 0-595-00089-4

Printed in the United States of America

In loving memory of my grandfather

PREFACE

A few years ago, I got an unsettling phone call: A stranger calling from cross-country claimed that my grandfather was also hers. Startled and skeptical as I was, her story somehow rang strangely true. So when she said that she was coming out West for a conference, and asked if I would like to meet her, I of course said, "yes."

When Judy and I met in San Francisco, she gently explained that my grandfather, a man revered in our community as among the most honorable of Jewish scholars and teachers, had, decades earlier, left a wife and two children for another woman—my grandmother!

Thus was planted the seed for *The Promised Hand*, a turn-of-the-century love triangle.

Some months later, I went back to New York, and Judy introduced me to her mother and aunt. My new aunts embraced me, though they had every reason not to. I interviewed them, and through them, their mother. I learned that my grandfather had kept in touch with his children from afar, secretly sending birthday greetings, holiday gifts and letters regularly. This, despite the community's face-saving fiction that he had passed away, that his first wife was a widow. The letters, in my grandfather's familiar hand and *schmaltzy* style, gave me goosebumps: They were so like so many letters he had written to me. Judy's mother photocopied these letters and gave them to me. She gave me photographs of the young family: herself as a little girl, a little boy, a smiling mom, and there was my Grandpa as the dad. They looked happy.

Additional research on life in the late teens through the '20s on the Lower East Side, and bustling Reno, Nevada, where my grandfather's first wife moved the family for a year, armed me with the backdrop I needed to present this story. Ultimately, I wrote this fictionalized history from the twin perspectives of Judy's grandmother and mine.

The fictional Isaac Grossman is a devoutly orthodox scholar and composer of Jewish liturgical music who abides by this code of honor: Revere your parents; respect your spouse; be mindful of the laws of the Lord. He loves Judaism deeply, as deeply as he comes to love an adoring girl he meets at the cinema, where he earns a wage playing the Wurlitzer to accompany the silent pictures. But his parents have promised him to another, in an arranged marriage typical of Eastern European immigrants to America. Whether to follow his faith or follow his heart is the struggle that Isaac confronts.

I hope you find the reading as pleasurable and interesting as I found the writing.

Susan Wolfe
Palo Alto, California

ACKNOWLEDGMENTS

This work would not have been possible, were it not for the generous interest and time invested by my long-lost, and new-found family members. I especially thank my cousin, Judith Merchant, who found me and befriended me, and introduced me to her side of the family.

Her late mother, Ruth Lichtenstein, of blessed memory, not only spent hours showing me around Brooklyn Heights and telling me about her childhood, she photocopied letters for me, reproduced family pictures, and corresponded with me as a true aunt. I deeply appreciate the support of Myron and Jetta Gordon, as well.

I was blessed to grow up in the shelter of my grandfather's love: a blessing that was denied Judy and her brother, Michael. My love and respect for my grandfather, of blessed memory, are profound: His influence, still, on my daily choices, my love of music, and my serious pursuit of the path of Judaism, are forever with me. Although this work may reveal a human frailty, it in no way diminishes my esteem for both him and my grandmother, who modeled Jewish family life for me, and for all of us blessed to be their grandchildren.

Finally, I wish to acknowledge my mother and father, my uncles and aunts, and all of my cousins who gave me the early foundation of family, as we gathered weekly, round the Sunday table at Grandpa's house.

BELLA

My father gave my virginity to a man I didn't know.

Afterward, I cringed in my corner of the bed, horrified by the spot of blood that penetrated my new white satin night gown—the one Mother gave to me wrapped in pink tissue paper, the one with lace trim on the collar and sleeves. Blood stained my new nightgown and stained the sheet, proving my innocence to the stranger snoring in bed beside me.

I was ashamed. I was sore. My flesh felt as though ants were trickling through my pores, and I wanted to go home, to the room that I shared with two of my five younger sisters. Alas, this musty three-room walk-up was to be my home forever more.

I lay still, staring at the ceiling and recalling the day's events, the events that brought me to this place.

*

Busy-making sisters and cousins and aunts bustled about the anteroom, oblivious to the emotional stirrings that left me quivering as visibly as any tangible demon could. Subconscious rage at my parents' choice—this was 1914 America, after all—excitement for what I believed would be the beginning of a new and better life, anticipation—and yes, apprehension—of the man I would meet at the foot of the aisle. Yet the people closest to me, those who I thought loved me best, went on with their silly preparations—pressing dresses, primping, preening—blind to my pathos; blind to me.

I searched the veiled face in the mirror. My broad, flat cheeks were flushed; my dark eyes shone brightly. With my black hair pulled back, sleek, in a twist, my face looked even wider than usual. Yet I felt hidden behind the veil. The longer the women, working, ignored me, the more I sensed that while I could make out their shadowy reflections through the lacy cut-outs in the veil, I remained invisible to them. They tittered, tinkered, told tales of their own weddings, past and future—insensitive, it seemed, to the fact that this, after all, was to be *my* day. The lilies they had lined up the aisles of the *shul* to mark the bridal way to the *chuppah,* the catering trays stacked in the kitchen, the *klezmer* band practicing music from the old country, the social hall banquet tables configured like a horseshoe with an invisible but inviolate line between the bride's and groom's seats to divide men from women—all of these arrange-ments—the very same arrangements that would be made *next* week for the *next* young couple to be wed—all of these were for *me* this day.

And yet, I felt absent, and empty inside, as if there was a hole in my belly the size of a beach ball.

*

To look at Isaac he seemed pleasant enough: Well-groomed and well-dressed (it was *his* wedding, too). He wore rimless glasses. He looked like a composer, hair lightly tussled, with long, slender fingers that contrasted with his compact, round shape. I imagined him on a piano bench inventing tunes for his brother's words. He was surprisingly short—five-foot-two at the most. How much more can you tell in a glance?

Though the guests arrived in couples, they split off at the sanctuary door. The women sat upstairs; the men below. I had heard of more liberal, new congregations that allowed men and women to sit side by side, but ours adhered strictly to tradition; our people had not been in New York that long. Our parents brought us when we were tots, from Russia, Rumania and the Ukraine. And although we were raised in New York City, our customs were rooted in the old country.

His palms were clammy, but his touch was soft when he placed the gold ring on my index finger. I searched his eyes for clues to his soul. Despite the supposed joy of the day, I thought that I sensed despair there. Or was he just as nervous as I was? I could not quite tell, but no matter about that. My mother said that his background was sound; that his family's friends were my family's friends. She said that he had been raised well, like me. She said we would learn to love each other.

He was a scholar. His special talents lay in music, and his ability to extract accomplishment from children. As devout an Orthodox Jew as I was, he devoted his skill to Hebrew education, composing liturgical music and children's holiday songs, organizing children's choirs, and staging musical theater shows. His family had little money, but once all eleven children were old enough to work, the family lived comfortably enough. Isaac and each of his siblings turned over their paychecks to their mother, an iron-willed woman who meted out money as sparingly as praise. She set the tone for the family; she, not Isaac's father, conveyed expectations, and moral values, the most important of which was the honor code that ruled our little neighborhood: Revere your parents. Respect your spouse. Be mindful of the laws of the Lord.

Crash! The glass shattered under Isaac's foot.

"*Mazel tov!*" yelled the guests in the congregation.

The lacy veil hid my child bride's tears.

*

Alone now, in the anteroom, eating. We had fasted all day, as custom dictates. Custom also dictated consummation at once, but instead we ate, as most of the couples of our age did. We ate—*mandelbrodt*, melon and fresh bananas—in silence. What was there to say? After all, I had only just met the man.

And what could he have known of me? That I was young and strong, perhaps; that my family stock was stable. We were *tallis* makers by trade, one of only two American companies that manufactured decorative prayer shawls. After I finished high school, my family sent me to millinery school. There, I learned the art of hat making, much of which translated to the fancy stitchery that our business called for. I worked for the family on and off. Now, though, I would work no more. I had just vowed to devote myself to Isaac's household; I had promised to be neither slothful nor idle. Though our families had tried to pair us according to our upbringings, our natures, and our interests, our marriage, in truth, was a simple case of economics. Who I was mattered not one whit.

We could hear the guests milling about, awaiting us in the banquet room. "Ready?" he asked, in his first word to me.

And off we went.

*

When they boosted me, in my chair, high over their heads, I thought that I would lose all that I had just eaten. I gripped the seat tightly while drunken members of our *shul* lifted and lowered me to the rhythm of the music. Help! I thought. But to whom could I call? My parents had given me to Isaac, a man I did not know well enough to ask for help.

The music quickened; the pace got frenetic. My stomach somersaulted as the dancers dipped and turned my chair.

I looked across the hall, to the circle of men supporting Isaac in the air. He laughed, he mocked them; these were his friends. He waved to me once, but he was absorbed by the fervor of the music, the moment.

He was, after all, a musician at heart. Why should he not revel in this rhythm? He seemed disappointed to return to our seats at the head of the hall, on display to our parents' guests. I, on the other hand, felt great relief.

We ate, we drank. He drank too much. His mother, seated on my side of the horseshoe, gave her son the evil eye. But still, he quaffed wine as if it were water. Apparently he liked to drink. Appparently, his brothers did, too. Red faced and breathless under hot top hats and coats, they maintained the merriment until, at last, the wine ran out, the guests said goodnight. And that was the end of our wedding party.

*

Which brings me here, to my nuptial bed.

Of course I was a virgin. How dare you even wonder? My experience consisted of shy smiles at boys and, if I was lucky, perhaps one in return— all, of course, under a chaperone's eye. I had not been permitted so much as a date, though some of the more modern families allowed it. Mine did not. I had already been promised to Isaac when I finally expressed an interest in boys, so what was the point in a date, after all? At dances I danced with other girls, drank punch with my parents, watched couples whose families had adopted the ways of the new world pair off. In school, as in synagogue, we sat separately: Boys on the left and girls on the right. In other words, we could look but we could not touch.

Now, in the darkness of this room, all of the rules instantly have changed.

He reaches for me, no tenderness left in his touch. He is still drunk and befuddled from wine. He fumbles, he squeezes, he hikes up my night gown, and I feel him groping between my legs. He foists his naked self onto me, and I feel his thumb pressing hard against my private parts. But no, of course, it is not his thumb.

Was I naive?

Was Mary's lamb white as snow?

AMALIA

If I didn't love him so much, I'd hate the bastard.

Where in the *hell* was his Goddamned backbone?

I was sure he'd pull out before today came.

He says he loves me, and I know he does. So why am I sitting in my old room, in my sister's house, alone?

I will, now, always be alone.

My parents are dead. My family is poor. My looks are average. Without a dowry, which we can't afford, no one will take me as a bride. My heart is pure; its one love is Ike.

We've been in love for four years now. We met at the movie house, where he plays the organ while the silent pictures run. One night after the show, he asked if he could walk me home.

I lived with my older sister and her husband, and their daughters, who were just a few years younger than I. My sister was old enough to have been my mother: She and Mama were pregnant together, though she lost the boy child she should have delivered around the time that I was born. When Mama died, my sister took me in and raised me right alongside her own two. And after my nieces, Rose and Gert, married, their new husbands moved into the house with us. My sister's family had no money: The single asset was the house. My sister offered it up as a dowry, and landed a couple of working-class husbands for her daughters. Well, at least the girls were married, she said. Well, at least the boys had a roof over their heads, the grooms' families said. I was lucky that they all agreed to let me stay. I had nowhere else to go, and besides, mine was an extra pair of hands to help with cooking, cleaning, washing clothes, bathing my nieces' babies and the like.

Ike changed my world. He told me I was beautiful in a way no other woman was. He went on and on about the curve of my breast, the broad

"S" of my shoulder to waist to hip, the strength of my jaw line, the gleam
in my eye. I know what you are going to say: That he was just handing me
a line. But somehow, from his lips, the words rang sincere. He made me
feel special, and I sensed an aura around me, glowing from within, especially after I'd been with him. He opened me up in the most wholesome of
senses. It didn't seem to matter whether we made physical love. Our every
interaction was love-making, whether walking or talking, shopping or skipping stones on a pond. We matched, and like book ends, or bed posts, or
candle sticks, once you'd seen us together it was hard to imagine us apart.

When he first told me his parents' plans for him, I laughed. Of course,
he would find a way out of this archaic holdover from the old country.
Arranged marriages, indeed! In 1914? In America?

Besides, we were practically living together—without a wedding yet—
but still, for all practical purposes we were engaged to be married. We spent
all of our spare time together—most afternoons, and even an occasional
night, when we thought we could get away with it, when I could manage to
sneak into Ike's house after his family had gone to bed, and sneak back into
my own bedroom before anyone in my sister's house was awake.

As for the passion, may I be indelicate? Just to look at him made me
wet. Our lovemaking was like none I've ever heard of or known: His touch
could tame me into submission, or tease me into a frenzied state. He knew
all of my most sensitive spots, and I believe I knew his, too. But it was a
funny thing about Ike, the thing that perhaps reveals most about him: He
seemed more gratified by indulging my pleasure than in any manipulation
I offered him.

Our bodies fit like two puzzle pieces, one's curves molding to meet the
other's. When we walked, my shoulder fit under his arm; his fingers
splayed comfortably between my ribs. Our minds matched in wit, in
spirit, in view. I always thought somehow, we'd find a way, for ours was a
love that made hearts sing, that lifted the souls of strangers we met. No
right-minded person would break it apart.

Alas, I was wrong.

Bella, naturally, knew nothing of us. She had never met me. She had never even met Ike. But I was sure that once she knew, she'd retreat from her parents' plans.

So, get this:

Ike refuses to tell her, out of reverence for his parents, he says.

His parents refuse to tell her. They gave their word to her family, they say.

His brothers refuse to tell her, out of respect for tradition, they say.

That leaves me, and Ike begs me not to tell her.

Their wedding day gets closer and closer, and he keeps saying he'll think of something. Meanwhile, he's getting fitted for a new suit to wear to his wedding, ordering a groom's hat, making plans to move from his family's home into a new apartment, in Brooklyn, *with her.*

They're probably already married by now, dancing and laughing, eating and drinking. Ike likes to drink. He likes to gamble and he likes to drink.

Damn the bastard!

I pound my fists on the pillows and cry.

*

I was just a schoolgirl when I met Ike, just on the cusp of womanhood.

I'd begun to fill out: My breasts pulled taut the buttons on the blouse of my school uniform and my short pleated skirt swept against the cap of my knee in a way unbecoming any decent young woman. I probably should have had a new uniform, but my family was poor, and there were babies to feed and clothe at home. I still tied a ribbon around my thick auburn hair in a swingy, shoulder-length ponytail. I still wore knee-socks and scuffed saddle shoes.

We passed notes in class when we weren't skipping out. I giggled with girlfriends and imagined boyfriends and read movie magazines in the drug store after school.

How I loved the movie queens! Their perfect features and sleek, statuesque figures provided a stark contrast to my prominent nose, my small, squinty eyes, my unruly hair and my short, *zaftig* shape. My hips and bust were big, but, at least, proportionately so. My legs were shapely, but short.

I spent many an evening at the movies, watching those gangly beauties dance across the screen, their flowing hair and flowing gowns attracting the kisses of leading men. I'd heard the boys in the audience whispering, wondering what it would be like to make love to such women. My rapture was based on a slight variation: I wondered what it would be like to make love *as* such women.

I was often the only girl at the show. Many of the others in our neighborhood were not allowed out in the evening alone. Their parents thought it improper to gad about unescorted at night. But my nieces and their new husbands were less concerned with my whereabouts than the daunting tasks of tending to aging parents and crying infants, so I was pretty much on my own.

Movie tickets cost a nickel, which I rarely had to spend. Most times I sneaked down the alley behind the theater and waited for the early show to let out. When the audience opened the exit doors, I slipped in, unnoticed, against the flow of traffic. The ushers were occupied in the lobby out front, escorting the next show's patrons to their seats, so I hardly ever got caught. On the rare occasion anyone looked askance at me, I pretended to be flustered, as though I had been on my way out when I'd discovered that I'd accidentally left something behind, and was now merely going back in to retrieve it.

Most nights I stayed until all the credits had rolled. I liked sitting in the dark, alone, listening to the Wurlitzer and waiting to see whether the organist, tonight, could time the end of his piece to the end of the film.

When the lights came up, the organist and I were often the only ones left in the house. We'd nod to each other, sometimes smile, and then go our separate ways at the door.

He was a bit older, a bit smoother, a bit more charming than the boys I had been allowed to date. I confess I sometimes fantasized about him, in much the same way I daydreamed about the stars. To me, he was an inextricable part of the movies, as untouchable as any of the Hollywood idols on screen.

So I was more than a little bit surprised when, one evening after the credits rolled, after the nod and the smile and all, he asked me out for coffee and cake.

*

He must not have noticed that I snuck into the theater. At least, if he did, he didn't say so. He flirted.

I thought he was baiting an awkward adolescent.

I wasn't very sophisticated, didn't care much for school, so there were only so many subjects that I could discuss. My only real interest was the movies, which made me an eager listener for him.

He spoke about screening each silent movie to select the accompanying music, timing his selections to dramatize each scene, trying to play to the director's intent. He talked about his own compositions, about the feeling he tried to convey in each piece, and how the liturgical lyrics made it easier for him to create meaning in the melody. He seemed to like talking about himself—about his large family, his brother, the rabbi, about his affinity for word games—so much so that he, politely, took no notice of me tugging at my hem, wishing that my skirt were longer, and fidgeting to pull my sweater around the bursting buttons at my bosom.

"So, *bella* Amalia," he chided me in an instantly manufactured Italian accent.

I was fourteen. I was enchanted.

"May I escort you home?" he asked in his own voice.

I took my last sip of coffee and nodded 'yes.'

*

We walked in step, with our hands in our pockets, and finally, as if to break the quiet, he asked, "What's your favorite song, Amalia?"

In the relaxed mode of our late night stroll, I wasn't thinking very fast, and, perhaps because I was so giddy over spending the evening with Ike, upbeat vaudeville tunes vamped in my mind's ear.

"*Take Me Out to The Ball Game*," I blurted.

"O.K., Slugger," he said. "I will."

*

I dared not tell my girlfriends that I'd met an older man. Many of them had older brothers who they'd tried to interest in me. And I still held out the hope, however small, that one would bite despite my many draw-backs—no dowry, plain looks, no family background. But I couldn't get Ike out of my mind. If I had thought I could get away with it, I'd have gone to the movies that night and the next and the one after that with the hope of bumping into him. But that would be too obvious. No one in our lower east side neighborhood could afford to spend a nickel a night at the picture show.

I took to walking home from school the long way, past the coffee shop we'd sat in until close to midnight the night we went out. I would peek in the window at our table, and, sometimes, make eye contact with our wait-ress, who came on duty at three o'clock sharp.

*

One day I saw Ike sitting there.

I blushed. I started to turn around. I looked away from the window, across the street. I heard a tap on the glass. I could hardly bring myself to look.

I kept walking.

I heard it again.

Rap-tap-tap.

I peeked.

He beckoned.

My heart skipped at the sight of him, my face flushed (attractively, I hoped). I smoothed my hair, I smoothed my skirt. Again, I wished that it were longer. I slipped into the doorway, dipped into my lip rouge and swiped my mouth, and pushed through the swinging glass door to join him.

"Haven't seen you at the movies lately," he said, casually.

"It's been the same picture for the last three weeks," I said.

"Oh. And I thought all this time you'd been coming to see me."

Gulp. What to say to a line like that?

"Well," I said in my most sophisticated voice. "Seeing you has always been like dessert."

"Have some," he said.

I blushed again, embarrassed. Maybe I'd seen too many movies. But then I remembered that he'd said he enjoyed double entendres, that he made a hobby of inventing them.

"Thanks," I said. I crinkled up my nose and nodded. "I'll have a milkshake."

*

That was in the spring, just before summer vacation from school.

I really had no definite plans. I figured I would find a job. But suddenly, every free moment was filled with Ike.

We picnicked in Central Park, window shopped on Madison Avenue, took the ferry to Staten Island, visited the Statue of Liberty.

In between, we talked—about our lives, our likes, our dislikes, our dreams—we touched—first with our hands, and, as we grew closer, with our heads and with our hearts. We related to each other on a level that encompassed the mind, the spirit and the soul.

At the end of the summer, my sister, my nieces, their husbands and babies went to the beach for a week's vacation.

I stayed in the city, presumably to work odd jobs, but also drawn to stay near Ike. A day without him was a day unfulfilled.

We had only one evening each week to go out. The rest of the nights he had to work. And since I neither wanted to appear too eager, nor could I afford a ticket, nor did I want him to know I snuck in, I stayed away from the movies on purpose. I hadn't seen a film in weeks.

That night, Ike said, he had a surprise for me.

He came by my house just before work, and asked me to come to the movies that night.

"I don't play as well when you're not there," he said. "Oh, and do me a favor, will you, Mal? I know you don't need it, but here," he passed me a ticket of admission. "Use a ticket this time? I don't want to bail you out of jail tonight. I rather hoped we could go out."

*

I didn't know what picture was playing, but I really didn't care.

Ike seated me in the theater, and took his place behind the Wurlitzer.

The house darkened, the film began and I began to laugh out loud.

It was a romance film, of course. They all were. But tonight the opening music didn't quite fit.

Only Ike and I understood the logic in introducing a romance with "*Take Me Out to the Ball Game.*"

*

I invited him into the empty house for coffee.

My pulse raced as I put the water up to boil. We had never shared this much privacy. Always, before, we'd been in public places.

The dishes clattered as, nervously, I tried to match the cups and saucers. I was on the kitchen step stool, reaching for the coffee canister on top of the metal cupboard when he clamped his hands around my waist, lifted me lightly off the step and gracefully spun me around to face him. In a single, fluid motion his open lips were on mine, his belly pressed against my own and I felt myself flush across the cheeks, beneath the arms, between the legs. His tongue gently teased the smooth, tender tissue inside my lips. His fingertips tickled the soft crease under my arm. I closed my eyes, enjoying the silky, soft, wetness of Ike's kiss.

"I've been wanting to do that for a long time," he whispered. And before he continued, he asked, "May I?"

"You may," I whispered. I squeezed his hand.

He led me to the couch, where he held me close and kissed me some more. His hands cupped my face now, stroked my cheek, my neck, glided down my chest and tenderly, naturally, swept across the curve of my breast, brushing back and forth, up and down. The glow he lit set me to tingling, and I was surprised—but not—to find myself both warm and wet.

I caressed his thigh, my hand instinctively moving higher.

The teapot whistled.

I got up, reluctantly, to make the coffee.

And then, without a word between us, he led me to my room.

*

"So, what did *you* do all week," my nosy niece, Rose, asked when the family returned. She was taunting me, so I decided to shock her with the truth.

"Ike and I made love," I said.

"You did *not!*" She was laughing.

"We *did.*" I was not.

"You *wouldn't!*" she said, accusingly.

"We would…We *did,*" I said defiantly.

"I don't *believe* you!" she charged.

So I gave up trying to explain the most beautiful moment I had known.

*

I had awakened with my head resting on his chest, my arm draped across his body. How absolutely perfect, I thought in the still of the dawn. My first experience, gentle and sweet, with someone I love, in the safe haven of my little-girl room, in my own bed, in my own house. I looked at the memories around the room: The teddy bear, matted from comforting me through storms of rain and storms of tears; the colorful hair ribbons tied around a fat pencil that poked out the top of my dresser drawer; the short-lived ballet slippers, now about three sizes too small, hanging from a nail in the wall.

I took up ballet in early adolescence. An uptown ballet school teacher had offered free classes for the immigrant girls in our neighborhood. Never mind that I wasn't an immigrant, at least, not a recent arrival. Anyway, something inside me craved the grace, the freedom, the evocative spirit of the prima ballerina. But the bulges emerging—all over my body, it seemed to me—rendered me far too awkward to dance. I was embarrassed by wearing the scant leotards that the instructor required, but I'd loved the sophistication of the satin slippers—even second-hand satin slippers—laced up my leg, the half-inch-wide ribbon shimmering as I walked.

I walked, but, as it turned out, I could not dance.

So why did I keep the toe shoes? Perhaps it was the promise they had offered before I even slipped them on. Perhaps they, like my movie pin-ups, were a symbol of what I wished I could be, but knew in my heart that I never would. Perhaps I was just too lazy to heave them.

The teapot was cold when we crept out to the kitchen.

I put it back on the stove again, but before it was hot, Ike was ready to leave.

"I hate to leave you," he cooed, brushing my cheek.

I didn't know why he had to go.

"I hope that there will come a day when we won't have to say good-bye," he said.

I looked into his eyes and nodded, yes.

BELLA

Isaac made love to me every Saturday, except, of course, when I was *niddah*—menstruating and therefore, unclean and unfit, by Jewish law, for physical contact with a man.

On the seventh day after my menstrual flow ended, I immersed myself in the community *mikvah*, and then, deemed purified by rabbinic and community standards, I was fit again for my wifely duty.

It was a *mitzvah,* a commandment to be fulfilled, just like lighting candles, blessing wine, breaking bread, and keeping kosher. I had grown accustomed to his way in our marital bed, which was quite satisfactory when he was sober, and sometimes even enjoyable.

In between our weekly lovemaking, we busied ourselves with our separate pursuits. After a dinner together and the requisite *benshing*—prayers praising God chanted after the meal—Isaac went to work most nights at the movie show. He spent the hours after his morning prayers at the composition bench. Afternoons he taught Hebrew classes and tutored remedial students and *bar mitzvah* boys. Mother wondered whether I was lonely, but I was just as happy to be allowed the time—not only to convert our apartment into a home, to concern myself with white paint and crisp slip covers, silver polish and elbow grease—but to enjoy my own pursuits. I joined a women's book club at *shul*, I volunteered my time to a society devoted to feeding the poor, and occasionally, I worked odd hours hand-stitching the specially ordered, detailed *tallisim* that our family business was known for producing.

It was a far happier life than I had feared fate handed me on my wedding night. Isaac was truly good to me. He complimented my cooking, undeservedly so. I was a newlywed novice, just learning my way around the kitchen, experimenting with friends' and relatives' recipes, and repeating the successes within less than a week. He praised my appearance—no small matter to a man who took great pride in his own. In fact, my father used to chide him about shopping uptown when our local, Jewish merchants needed all of our support. But to no avail. Isaac insisted on a crisp, polished finish, available only, he assessed, from the very best, uptown haberdasheries. He kissed me as he came and went. He said that he loved me. I believe that he did.

Isaac was scrupulously meticulous. He kept one room of our flat for his den. Everything was in its place. Even the insides of his desk drawers were exact: He lined up a row of erasers along the seam of the top center drawer. Behind them he placed his pencils, side by side, according to length. Bounding the other side of the pencils were two oblong boxes that kept them from rolling: One contained paper clips, the other held tacks. The bulk of the drawer held carbon copies of his every correspondence, dated and stacked chronologically, with the latest one on top. When the number of carbons reached twenty-five, he stored them, by date, in an accordion file that took up most of his bottom right drawer. He was an avid letter writer.

The inside of the piano bench was no less orderly than his desk: Sheet music, sorted alphabetically, by composer, stacked on the left as you lifted the lid; books of composers' collected works on the right. Above, on the music stand, he kept a book of Beethoven sonatas, a single, finely sharpened pencil, and a pad imprinted with blank musical scores on which he made note of fresh melodies as they struck him.

His routine was predictable. Isaac awoke around seven, wrapped himself, hand and head, in *tefillin* for his morning prayers, then made coffee, and even brought me a cup in bed. He bathed and he dressed, and by nine o'clock he was on his way. He spent his mornings working on compositions, usually in concert with his brother, Israel, sometimes at Israel's apartment downstairs, and sometimes at the nearby *shul*, where Israel was the head rabbi. Some time before two he went to the *talmud torah*, where he tutored boys training for *bar mitzvah*. He came home between five and six o'clock. We talked, we ate, we *benshed* together. Then, by seven, he left for the theater. He came home late, after I was asleep. He really was quite industrious at stringing together a livelihood.

As for my own day-to-day activities, I found my way to housewifery, and took to it rather well, I would say. Each morning I addressed a different room—cleaning, painting, straightening, decorating—or laundered the clothes, or changed the bed linens. Afternoons I met friends for coffee and cake, or sometimes, for cards. Our book group met one afternoon each month to discuss a book that each of us had read. I spent many afternoons traversing the busy marketplace—storefronts with awnings and old men with pushcarts—picking out yarns and fabrics, threads and knick-knacks for my various sewing projects, and fresh foods for supper, for me and Isaac. We ate together every night. I made it my practice to make a nice meal: A salad, a main dish, a starch, a dessert. Always, there was fresh bread with dinner. Always, a glass or two of wine. Afterward, when he went to his night job, I was left to myself again.

I loved to read, especially plays. With so much time to myself—far more than most young brides—I had wandered my new neighborhood, discovered the New York Public Library branch, and in it, the works of William Shakespeare. I started reading them to ease my evening boredom. They were entertaining, filled with love affairs, duels, and melodrama. In them I also discovered Shakespeare's fresh and colorful plays on words. I knew that Isaac enjoyed word games, and I began to make lists of the ones I had found with the hope that, when we found time to talk on the weekend or on his night off, that I would have something of substance, if not scholarship, to contribute to the conversation. It was at the library that I met one of the women from synagogue, browsing in the fiction stacks. It was she who invited me to join the book club, where I was challenged to read, and gained new insights into literature from the others in the group.

I had only a high school diploma, and a year-and-a-half of millinery school, and though I rarely made my own hats, I always sewed my own clothes. They looked far better than store-bought. Like most of the girls my age, and my station, there was not much point in aspiring to more education than high school. We were already promised to husbands unknown: Our schooling served to fill the time until they were ready to marry us, and our life's merit would be measured by the families we raised.

So it was with mixed emotion—after only fourteen months of marriage—that I found myself a week overdue. I had hardly adjusted to married life; now it appeared, a child might be on the way. But it was still much too early to tell, and much too soon to tell anyone. So I tried my best to conduct business as usual. But I could not get babies out of my brain!

AMALIA

Even though he had married, we saw each other every day. He had appointments with students in the afternoon and he had to work at the movies at night, but his mornings, unbeknownst to Bella, remained relatively free, for me. So we had continued to see each other, to love each other, to plan and plot a future together.

He had become so much a part of each day, that when he told me he was leaving me, the initial months of loneliness assaulted me more severely than illness: I vomited almost everything I ate; I suffered from dysentery, too. The body he had celebrated as "voluptuous," even "juicy," shriveled to a skeleton. The mind he praised as fanciful, witty, street-smart and sincere went first numb, then dead, like a limb awither with gangrene.

And as with an amputated limb, I suffered phantom pains—my mind forgetting momentarily that Ike, who I had taken for granted as part of myself, was no longer, and never again would be mine. Mornings I still eyed myself in the mirror, still selected lacy, matching undergarments, still pulled my hair up, in the way that Ike always complimented. I still stood at the window, waiting and watching as if any moment he would come, walking spryly, round the corner to my door.

Reality ripped my heart from my chest.

Any spark Ike had seen in me was extinguished; any ember of life that burned in me was doused. I busied myself with household work, making myself a maid to my nieces, in back payment for my room and board.

I couldn't stand to leave the house, and did so only in absolute necessity. Tears welled up in my eyes on the street, in stores, any time I passed a place we had been, heard a song that we had heard together. I didn't want to see anyone I knew. I didn't want to make small talk. I didn't want my body touched; the thought of even a handshake or casual embrace stiffened my spine and turned me cold.

I lost the will to live, but lacked the courage to execute my death wish.

Circumstances forced me to confess that life was not to be the heady adventure I'd flirted with, but a survival test to be endured. I had partaken of love-induced highs, and now I was suffering the after-effects. The heart-break of the lowest lows tormented and twisted my head, my heart and my digestive tract. I writhed inside, so overcome with anguish that I wished nothing more than to slip off the planet, into obscurity. Alas, I knew that, even if I fled, I'd not find peace, for the enemy taunting me thrived within. So, at night, I prayed I would not wake to face another day of agony.

I spent most of my time in my room, alone, the same room where we'd first made love. I sometimes lay on my bed at night, touching myself the way he had touched me, bringing myself to ecstasy, and then lamenting that what I wished for would forever remain an unattainable, inexpress-ible, undeniable dream. I could not do for myself what he had done for me—not physically or emotionally or mentally or spiritually.

It was on such a night that it dawned on my why the ballet slippers still hung, limp, on the nail stuck into my bedroom wall. I had wanted, with a passion, to dance through life: To laugh and love and live lustily. With Ike, I had tasted life at its best.

Without him, now, I realized that the overriding lesson I learned in dance class was, sadly, metaphorically true: My fate would be to plod through life, never to grace the ballroom floor.

BELLA

I had missed two periods already. And yet, I hesitated to tell Isaac.

He seemed so busy. He arose early; he rushed off to work. He even seemed to be hurrying his daily prayers, supposedly a time of joy, wrapping the straps of the *tefillin* around his hand and his head by rote, and racing through a mumbled devotion to God. He worked three jobs to eke out our living, and never once lamented it. His mornings, he worked for himself, composing, though he rarely shared a work in progress with me. His perfectionism prevailed: I saw only the polished, published pieces. They were few and far between. His afternoons, he spent teaching and tutoring. His nights, he played at the movie house. All, without a peep of complaint. All, without a touch of bitterness. All, with energy, good spirit, and affection—for me, as well as for the work.

He turned his money over to me. Perhaps his mother was the source of this habit: She had demanded that he hand over his income to her before we married. I, on the other hand, never asked him for money. I had the money my family gave us from time to time, though I never flaunted it. Isaac had stated early on that he wished to be the sole support of our household, and that we should use my family fund as savings. But after that early pronouncement, he never questioned where the money went, never asked more than pocket change for himself, never gave me cause to worry.

Yet I did.

What would a baby do to our life?

I was still just getting to know my new husband, still marveling at his creative spark and wondering where he found his verve. I was still only surface-scratching his psyche, and, as though he was a character in a book, I hoped to unravel his complexities from afar. I wondered what motivated him, what he loved and what he despised, and what he would give his life to protect, all, through mere observation. It would be improper to ask such questions directly.

A baby would consume all my time, I knew, from the number of friends I had lost to motherhood. I saw none of the ones who had given birth. They were eaten, whole up, by tiny creatures so adorable it was hard to believe they could be so demanding. And yet, even as I contemplated the inability to continue my quest to know the man I married, a part of me felt happy: I believed that I was born to perform this function.

Each morning, I awoke, nauseated, lifted the neck of my night gown up to my eye, and peeked down at my churning belly. Was there any sign of it? Could Isaac tell if he looked close, if he touched? Did I show beneath my clothes? How long should I wait before I said something? I did not want him to guess it first.

I padded out to the kitchen and scoured the cupboards until I found where I had hidden the soda crackers. I took a stack of them back to the bed, and lay there, slightly propped up on the pillows, shaving off little bits with the fronts of my teeth, the salty crumbs piling onto my tongue like so much sawdust heaped round a sawmill. It neutralized the rancidness in my mouth and eventually, the acid in my stomach, until I could make my way to the bath.

Hard, hot water beating over my legs served to divert my dis-ease, for the moment. I could have spent all day in the bath, lying flat, with my feet positioned just under the faucet. I loved the beating, water pellets pounding against my shins. It was the one time of the day that I could forget I was two, that there was another being growing within me. I sat up to splash my face. Then I turned off the water, lay back again, and soaked beneath the water's surface.

When, finally, I pulled the plug from the drain and stepped out of the tub, I stood for a long time in front of the mirror, examining my belly's curve. Did it protrude so much more than before? I thought so, but could not tell for sure. Were my breasts really fuller, more tender, more pink, or was it just that I knew that they should be? My waist seemed thicker, and even my thighs and my buttocks seemed larger, looser, in proclamation of the event to come.

Stop it, I said to myself as I toweled dry. It is too early to tell, too early for wishes of what might come to be.

I allowed myself to fantasize about the wonder of new life: A small and cuddly creature of my very own, to have, to hold, to raise, to love, to teach the ways of our people to, and to enjoin me, forever and irrevocably, with Isaac; the smell of babies, their teeny feet and hands, the clothing even too small for dolls. The joy of such thoughts brought tears to my eyes, yet I dared not let them fall.

I pulled on my petticoat. It was tight at the waist. On came the dark dress, the black stockings and shoes.

I notched my belt on the loosest hole, buried my face in my hands and, for no reason that I could explain, I wept.

AMALIA

I heard from friends and family of Ike.

It ate me up that he was fine, functioning—indeed, flourishing—in his professional life, and, by all appearances, his personal life, too. He had published a book of liturgical music in the months since he had left me. What's more, he was, it seemed, the quintessential happily married man. They went dancing, I heard from friends, even touching, with apparent affection, in public. They went to the beach, to the theater and more, all with arms alink and faces aglow. But what sickened me most was imagining the two of them together in bed. How could he find satisfaction there, when I thought that what we'd shared was inimitable?

There was one time I ran into him. I suppose I secretly had hoped that sometime or other I would see him again. I fantasized that if we could share just one look, we'd throw ourselves together again, overcome with passion, with love, with relief.

Now, I wish it had never happened. He pulled the scab off the wound that I'd hoped, by now, was just a scar. I stood on the sidewalk outside the drug store, answering an acquaintance's "hello." It was my bad luck to run into someone I knew—funny, that now I don't even remember who. I only agreed to go to the store to pick up a prescription for my niece, who was ill. And then, out of the drug store walked Ike.

"Oh," he said, off balance. "Uh, well, how nice to see you, Mal. How have you been?"

And before I could say "fine" he was halfway down the block.

I could only speculate about his emotion. He must have looked at me, and wished, as I so often did these days, that I would simply go away. I instilled guilt, not by choice, but by my very existence. There was a people-pleasing side of him; he hated nothing so much as to disappoint others, to let down the people in his life. Seeing me, and my hurt, I know, caused him pain. And that, in turn caused me more anguish.

He had an important place in this community. He organized children's choirs, staged musical and Yiddish theater productions, trained the children in Judaica and Hebrew, tutored the *bar mitzvah* boys. All that, in addition to composing holiday and liturgical music. I, on the other hand, had nothing holding me here—no husband, no job, no parents to tend. Believe me, if I'd had anywhere else to go, I would have run like a bandit.

What was there for me to look forward to? No promise of marriage, no children to raise. No profession, no passion, no reason to live.

Some call it limbo. Some call it purgatory. Whatever it's called, you can take it from me, it's a God-forsaken place to be.

BELLA

"A child!" he exclaimed with joy, and I was glad not to deny it.

His eyes flashed, his lips parted to expose his broad teeth, a tear welled up in his left eye, and trickled down its outside corner.

He lifted me by my thickening waist and joyfully, gleefully whirled me around the room, my skirt flaring out in a hoop around me.

Then, abruptly, apologetically, he put me down.

"But I should be more careful with you. You're in a delicate condition. Oh, Bella, Bella! How I have *ached* for a family! This is the greatest news ever! I could sing a song! I could *write* one! I will!"

He sat down at the piano and plunked out a ditty. He was so comfortable there, in front of the keyboard. He took his new tune and transformed it into a medley of distinctive nationalities—a Jewish song at its heart, played in a Chinese motif, then Indian, Italian, French, Calypso. Then, turning more serious, he reworked the same melody, playing it first the way that Bach might have done, then as Beethoven might have expressed the music, and then, lightly, fiendishly, as Mozart.

My husband was truly talented.

I had never seen Isaac so giddy.

*

He barely left my side after that, always at the ready with an arm to steady me, always helpful, supportive, even doting.

He stayed home with me in the mornings, suddenly taking what he called a voluntary sabbatical from the rigors of his composing schedule. We blocked out where the nursery furniture would go. We shopped for fabrics and blankets and rattles. We pretended how it would be to have a baby in the house. Whether to sleep in a cradle or crib became a pressing and regular topic for discussion. We giggled about the silliest things: Isaac did impressions of sad cries and hungry cries and wet cries and cries of joy, making me laugh until my belly ached. We drew up an extensive layette wish-list; we made list after list of boys' and girls' names, marking the ones we liked with stars and crossing off the ones we did not, then changing our minds and tearing them up and making the lists all over again.

He came home earlier at night.

In bed, he snuggled up behind me, wrapped his arms around my middle, pressed his thighs up, beneath my seat, and hummed calming tunes, or whispered gentle thoughts to help quiet my mind, to help me to sleep. Sometimes, he nibbled the back of my neck, ever so gently, so tenderly. Slowly, all of my insecurities dissipated: I knew in my soul that this was love.

Overnight, it seemed, we had reached a new stride, and all because a baby was due.

Had I known that it would be this way, I would never have hesitated to tell him the news. When I told him I had been reluctant to tell him when I first suspected that I was expecting, he laughed.

"Bella," he said. "I knew before you did."

"What are you talking about?" I said, taking quick stock of my ever-changing shape.

"No, no. Not there," he said, lifting my chin up off of my chest. "The eyes. I could see it in your eyes."

"See what?" I was skeptical.

"Your eyes turned green, with yellow rings. It could only have been one thing," he said.

"Oh, Isaac!" I threw a pillow across the sofa at him.

He cuddled up beside me. We hugged.

I would never have imagined our life could be this blithe, and I reveled in it—while it lasted.

*

The months wore on; the novelty wore off.

I grew large, ungainly. I could not stand the sight of myself.

Yet for his part, Isaac made me feel like a princess. He could not have found my shape any more appealing than I, but he adored me as never before, told me that I glowed, that my belly was beautiful, that, even if I looked this way always, he would stay forever in love with me. He tried to hug me, but his arms were too short; when he tried to hold me in bed, I flopped one way or the other, unable, now, to balance on my side. Yet, somehow, he made it all all right. He would massage my middle, both front and back, cooing to the child inside me.

He said he was sure we were having a girl: God would not make only one like me. And he hoped, he said, for the sake of future generations, that the baby would be my replica.

*

How I wish he could have seen her when our baby daughter was born. She was a beauty; black hair styled in a little pixie, black eyes shining like an imp. Even before she was washed and swaddled, I found myself madly in love with her. She was petite—just under six pounds, and healthy in spite of her rapid ride out.

*

We had been taking an evening stroll around the block when I felt a trickle between my legs. I had heard, of course, that late in confinement, one can lose control of one's delicate functions. As indiscreet as incontinence is, I was rather enjoying our walk, and so asked Isaac to wait on the stoop while I went inside to change into dry undergarments. We were not ten steps from our front door when I found myself quite drenched again.

"You don't suppose…" I said to Isaac.

"Well, it could be," he answered.

"Perhaps we had better go to the hospital, just to be safe," I suggested, suddenly uncharacteristically meek.

The nurse in the labor and delivery department used an inch-long strip of litmus paper to test my trickle's acidity: Depending on the color that the litmus paper turned, the water would be deemed either urine or amniotic fluid.

Within minutes, we learned it was the latter.

"Any contractions yet, Dear?" the nurse asked me.

"No, at least not that I know of," I said.

"Oh, you'd know, Honey." She gave me a look that assured me I would.

"Anyway, in that case, there's no reason for you to stay here," she said. "Come back when the contractions begin, or, if they don't, then come on back in the morning."

When we got home I sat quietly on the couch, having grown quite contemplative.

"One way or another, we will be parents tomorrow," I said, waiting to glean Isaac's reaction to the imminent, permanent change to our lives.

But Isaac was bustling about nervously. I wondered what was on his mind.

"Bella." he said. "Darling." he said. "There are just a few things I need to take care of at the school, before the baby comes, because then, of course, I won't be going in for a few days. I just want to leave everything in order for my pupils, so they don't fall behind in their lessons, and so that none of them—or their parents—feels abandoned."

"What do you mean, Isaac?" I asked.

"I'll be right back," he said, avoiding my eyes.

"Isaac. We are about to have a baby. You heard the nurse: My contractions could start at any time. This is no time to leave."

"I promise you, Bella, I'll be right back," he said. And he walked out the apartment door.

*

Two hours later Isaac still was not home. My womb had begun to cramp rhythmically, regularly. In between pains I waddled down the hall to my neighbor's flat, to ask her to help me to the hospital.

My labor was easy—just seven hours between the first contraction and delivery—and I have a very high threshold for pain. It took just three pushes to push out our daughter. It was love at first sight. She was the most beautiful baby I had ever seen.

By late afternoon when Isaac finally showed up, with flowers, I was so much in love that I forgot all about being left on my own in the hours of impending maternity.

*

No one can prepare you for motherhood. No words can describe the sleep deprivation, nothing can console the let-down, the depression, and no one can express how consuming this love is.

As much as I loved her, I wanted to teach her to love, too. So I named her Ruth, with the hope that she, like Ruth, would be faithful, hard-working and generous—a friend, not only to me, to *us*, but to all whom she met: True to her family, her friends, her husband, herself.

Between Ruth and Isaac I was busy round the clock. I nursed her, I rocked her, I put her to sleep. I washed baby clothes and hung out baby clothes and folded baby clothes before she awoke for another feeding, another burping. A bath, a nap and it was time for me to prepare Isaac's dinner. He still expected the three-course meal, and I was determined not to fail. This was part of our formula for marital bliss; I would not forgo it   not even for sleep, which I desperately needed.

But, without my taking much notice, the seeds of resentment began to sprout. The rings made my eyes look like a raccoon's; I washed, but lacked the time to groom; the right shoulder of my every blouse was stained with spit-up that would not wash out; and I still wore maternity skirts: The rest were too tight, and I could find no time to sew.

Within a few days of bringing Ruth home, Isaac had returned to his pre-pregnancy routine: Out the door early and home very late. But there was no such order to my day: Every time I thought I had figured out the baby's eating and sleeping schedules, they changed. She was unpredictable.

When I complained of this to Isaac, he told me we would learn to prize her strong will, that unpredictability was an asset he respected.

Spooning a tablespoon full of mashed potatoes straight from the serving bowl into his mouth, he spoke, as he sometimes did, with his mouth full.

"Look, no one will ever grow bored with *her*, eh?"

Sometimes, lately, his comments cut me, and I wondered if he intended the double meanings that I inferred. I attributed my sensitivity to lack of sleep, to irritability. There were plenty of reasons why things were not perfect.

Frankly, I was too tired to fret.

*

He began to complain about his bread-and-butter work—the work that paid the bulk of his salary—not his composing in the mornings, but his afternoons across town. He said he disliked the distance, he disliked the tedium of teaching the same lessons over and over again with each new crop of twelve-year-olds. He disliked jostling for a seat on the commute-crowded streetcar to come home for dinner, eat and *bensh* quickly and dash down to the cinema.

Lately, he disliked coming home at all.

I admit that things were in disarray. Ruth had set my timing off. I was no longer the meticulous homemaker he had married. Now, my clothes were ill-fitting, my appearance unkempt. I lacked the time—and frankly, the will—to pull myself together for him—to apply make-up and to arrange my hair. I no longer had the time to read, which dulled our infrequent conversations considerably. The house itself was strewn with bottles, blankets, rattles and diapers. I could not seem to get any-thing done. Even dinner was sometimes late, or lacking. Often, the baby was wailing when he walked through the door; often, I felt like crying with her—out of loneliness, frustration, despair. I could not blame him for staying away; I did not want to be there myself.

*

After Ruth, our sex life waned. In the beginning, Isaac said nothing. Some months later, he explained that he had not yet rekindled our weekly union out of consideration for the strain my body had undergone in childbirth, and for my weariness due to new motherhood. He said that he wanted to afford me every possible opportunity to rest. But in truth I believe that both of us knew the real reason the flow of our lovemaking had ebbed: For lack of enthusiasm on his part and mine.

I tried to reignite the spark despite my persistent state of exhaustion. I suggested one night a week out of the household routine, and Isaac enthusiastically agreed. But on the night that we had set aside—after the neighbor had arrived to look after Ruth, and I had done up my hair and put on a new dress—I waited and waited, embarrassed, exhausted, and finally, hours later, went to bed alone. Isaac never came for me. He had misinterpreted my suggestion for a night out together as a night out for him, and a night off for me. Isaac's night out soon became two a week, and then, some months later, grew into three without him at my table. He rarely came home before two in the morning, and when he came in his breath smelled of bourbon and cigarettes. He barked that there was nothing improper in taking a drink to unwind after working three jobs every day.

The work began to wear on him. He forgot the simplest things, even the things that I had hoped would bring back the joy between us: The baby's monthly birthday, which I had set aside for celebration; family occasions I had asked him to attend. He even became forgetful about his paperwork, shuttling across town for papers forgotten at the *talmud torah* almost every weekend, now.

Poor dear!

But just when I stopped expecting anything from him, he would surprise me with chocolates, with flowers, with perfume. The gifts seemed to assuage whatever guilt I imagined he felt, though I surely did nothing to inflict any guilt on him. I did not blame him for his own distraction; not in the least. He was terribly overburdened. And where I had been able to devote myself fully to him before Ruth, I now had my own preoccupation.

AMALIA

"Take me back," the last line begged.
I sat on my bed and reread the letter.

October 3, 1916

Dear Amalia,

It seems like an eternity.

Over these many months, I have imagined you, alternatively, in two ways: In one scenario I see you, strong, independent, with no need and no use for a man like me. Indeed, I imagine you may be quite angry, and rightly so. But in my fantasy, I hope to return to find you still as forgiving of heart, as lusty in spirit, as in love with me as I am, still, and always, with you.

Oh, I tried to forget the magic we shared. I tried to focus on my marriage, which, I believe, would have been good enough, were it not for knowing and missing how good life can be—with you. I tried to trick myself into enhancing my relationship with my wife, to give the marriage every chance to succeed: Every time I saw your favorite flowers, I bought them for you, but gave them to her. Every time I thought of a special night out for us— a concert, or an evening awhirl on a ballroom floor—I imagined you but invited her.

But after nearly a year of trying, I have to conclude that our love—yours and mine—is a once-in-a-lifetime occurrence. It cannot be replicated with anyone else.

It is unfortunate that the measure of love must, so often, be loss. I tried to ignore the loss, to numb myself to the pain. For the most part I did an adequate job. But in recent months I find myself in your neighborhood, on your street, walking by your house, and hoping to catch a glimpse of you at the door, a peek at you through the window. And each time I do not, another bit of my heart flitters away like so many ashes from the hearth.

I don't know that I can offer you all that you want, all that you deserve, but even a thin slice of life beats no life at all. And without you, my angel, I feel dead inside.

Will you see me, Mal?

Take me back.

With eternal and increasing love,

(Your) Isaac E. Grossman

The paper rattled against my shaking hand. My heart pounded. I wanted to scream out, 'Yes!' With each passing month without him, I had become more and more convinced that it was absolutely, completely and finally over, that Ike had found happiness with someone else. Yet deep in the crevasses of my soul, in the place where inner wisdom abides, I held onto a speck of impossibility, wishing nightly on a star that somehow, some way, he would come back.

Now that it appeared he had, I felt, suddenly, self-protective. In recent weeks my health had improved. Although I still ached inside with loss of love, I'd stopped throwing up, and I'd put on some of the weight I had lost. I'd begun, just begun, to venture out of the house, to spend snippets of time with very close friends over coffee and cake. Would seeing him again propel me into a relapse? And how could I cope if he left me again?

I stretched out on the bed and closed my eyes. I pictured our wedding—different now than before. I walked down the aisle with my great nephews beside me; their mothers (my nieces) occupied the front row. I wore a street-length dress, not a long one, fitted at the bodice down to a drop waist, with white pumps that had a pearl on each toe.

Ike wore a dark suit. No tuxedo for him. One brother stood with him as his best man. Another brother, the rabbi, conducted the ceremony. Only family—no friends—were in attendance.

I opened my eyes.

Oh, fantasy!

Ike was already married, to somebody else. For all I knew they had a child, even two. What was it he meant to offer to me?

I looked at the letter for a third time. His penmanship looked almost machine-generated: So consistently straight up and down, with no slant, just the occasional underlined word and a curlique beneath his signature—for emphasis, but also for aesthetics: He placed great importance on how things looked.

I looked for specifics in the letter this time: What, exactly, was the proposal? Yet there were none there, not even a suggested meeting time and place.

The script was his; the words were his; the sentiment, I recognized as his. But he had left himself an out. He hadn't really come to me: If I wanted him back, the next move was mine.

*

I wanted to believe in horoscopes and fortune tellers, for if they could be real, then fairy tales might be, too.

I was still wishing on stars, reading tea leaves, consulting palm readers and tarot cards when Ike simply and naturally reentered my life: One morning I heard a knock at the door, and when I opened it, there he was, on the step.

"Hi," he said, shyly.

I smiled, in spite of myself, but said nothing.

"I hope you got my letter," he said.

"Yes, yes I did," I answered him.

"Good. Well, then, I wonder whether you might like to join me for a walk?"

"I'll get my sweater," I said. "Wait here."

Tentatively, but, oddly, quite naturally, too, he slipped his arm around my shoulders, and I felt mine wrap around his waist. We squeezed.

"Hi," he said, softly, searching my eyes for response.

"Hi," I whispered, with some hesitation.

We walked a few blocks in silence, then we walked a few more. We rounded a corner. He pushed me into the recessed doorway of a shop that was closed. He backed me up against the brick wall, tipped my chin up to his lips, and sweetly, gently kissed my mouth. My arms stretched around his neck, my hips arched forward to push against his, and I answered his gentle kiss with ferocity, with the appetite of one who has gone hungry too long.

He pawed my cheek, he pawed my neck, he pawed my shoulder, he pawed my breast. I pumped my hips, and let my hand slip between his legs, where I kneaded his inner thigh, careful to avoid initiating anything he might yet reject.

After a few moments, I stopped myself.

I placed my palm against Ike's chest, unlatched our lips and looked in his eyes.

"What does this mean?" I asked him, sincerely.

"I'm back," he said, not hiding his pleasure.

"Yes, I see that," I said. "But what exactly does that mean?"

The smile fell off of Ike's eager face.

"Why don't we get some lunch and talk," he said.

*

"I have a child," he told me over sandwiches and milk. "I have a responsibility to her, and to her mother. But my heart will always belong to you."

"That's fine, Ike," I said, surprised at my calm, surprised at my reserve. "So what do I do with that piece of knowledge?"

Perhaps I sounded slightly sarcastic.

"I love you, Mal. I've never stopped loving you. I never will stop loving you. I can't. You're in me. We share the same heart, we share the same soul. When I'm without you, I'm only half a man. I cannot fathom enduring a life that doesn't include you."

"So what do you intend to do with me?"

"I intend to love you, to keep loving you, to take care of you as well as I know how."

"Ike, how can you care for a wife and child, and for me, too? What exactly do you propose?"

"I propose," he said, taking a breath, "I propose a life-long love affair. If circumstances should change over time, you have to know that I'll beat a path straight to your door. For the time being, my obligation has to rest there, but my heart's only resting place is here."

"I see."

I finished my sandwich. Ike paid the bill. Then we clasped hands and caught a cab.

*

He took my hand.

We took a room.

He turned the deadbolt with one hand and pulled me, by my blouse, slowly toward him with the other. His nimble fingers skillfully released me from my street attire. The lace beneath my open blouse invited him to test his touch, to tease the delicate skin beneath with fingertips so tender that I felt the effects of their exploration not only between my breasts, but between my legs, too.

He unfastened my belt. He unzipped my skirt. The pleats encircled my feet on the floor.

The bare flesh above my mid-thigh quivered. I wondered whether the magic remained.

"It looks as though I'm falling behind," I whispered, unloosening his tie.

I nearly ripped his shirt buttons off, eager to stroke the breadth of his chest, to feel his heart right next to mine.

He, too, was desirous; he unnotched his own belt and guided my hand from his chest to his waist.

I dropped to my knees, first kissing his chest, then his abdomen, as I unhitched his trousers and watched them fall to his ankles. I clasped my hands around him, burrowing, and the elastic waistband of his undershorts brushed my face as I slid it down, past his thighs, past his knees, down to the floor. Then he was in my mouth, warm and soft, growing longer, stiffer, sleeker, becoming the object of my every fantasy.

"God!" he groaned.

His every utterance was a sigh, a groan, a breathy whisper.

I bobbed my head forward and back, sliding him in and out of my mouth, then flicking the tip of my tongue against the ridge on the sensitive underside. As engaged as I was, he seemed even more so.

He placed his hands beneath my arms and pulled me to my feet again. He stepped out of his pants; I stepped out of my skirt. He backed me up toward the bed and gently lowered me onto it.

He took great care in unfastening each garter and gliding each silky-soft stocking down my leg, off my foot, and folding each, delicately, on the desk. He slipped off my panties, and scooted me back to the middle of the mattress. Then, gracefully, he plunged inside me.

In that single instant, the time between us vaporized; like so much water in a boiling pot, it discreetly and indetectably vanished.

*

That's how the love that lifted spirits, that made the hearts of strangers smile, became a dirty little secret—a tawdry affair like any sneaky, seedy, low-rent sex thing. We used friends' apartments, we made love in the park, a splurge for us was a cheap hotel, paid for with winnings from Ike's backroom gambling. But even horrid surroundings could not dim our light, our forever and ever affair of the heart.

It wasn't all sex, after all.

He was my best friend, my confidante, *and* my lover.

Now, in addition to mornings, we would meet late at night.

We'd sit in a club, where we'd drink and we'd talk over the noisy background music. Many a night he slipped into the back room where some of the men played high-stakes poker. Ike was in no financial position to play, but he could bluff like nobody's business. When he lost he wrote out IOUs; when he won, he stashed the winnings away from Bella, to be used for a trinket for me, a shared fancy meal and the very occasional room-by-the-hour. Sometimes I watched him, sipping a drink, but most times I didn't. The other men didn't like me hanging around, and I think I made Ike a little bit nervous. He didn't lie very well around me, and lying was the name of this game. So I drank in the lounge while he drank at the card table, and the drunker we were when we reconvened, the more we opened up, and the more that we learned about each other's daily lives.

He, of course, had one: A career, a home, a wife and a child. I, on the other hand, did not. I spent my time tending others' concerns; neither my home nor my family were my own. I had no place to mark as mine. Not even my lover belonged to me.

Don't misunderstand: I knew right from wrong. But I lost myself so completely in Ike, that even when my conscience plagued me—grabbed me by the throat, reminded me that I was breaking God's law, told me that I was sacrificing my character, debasing my very existence—even then I could not keep myself from falling more and more deeply each time we were together.

He was a romantic, an utter dreamer. He hoped, he wished for a fateful intervention. "Somehow, some way," were his watchwords. But he was unwilling to take the steps necessary to bring us together legitimately—an inaction that infuriated me.

Yet each time I was ready to break things off—and there were many along the way—each time, he'd captivate me, cultivate me, wrap me under his spell, and I would lose my resolve, resolving instead to wait, to hope, to try to believe, for I knew that without him I had been as close as I want to be to death.

You cannot force someone to love you your way; you cannot force someone to uproot himself. So what other conclusion could I draw? As much as I hated to admit it to myself, I knew, too well, my answer to the question, are you better off with him or without him?

BELLA

The hints had been there all along, but I chose to overlook them.

Now, as I stacked up incidents and inconsistencies, reviewed eccentricities and excuses, I could ignore the apparent facts no longer.

He had taken to frequenting the theater, he said, though when he could go I did not know. He worked every night except the one he was home, and the matinees were on *Shabbos*, when our family attended *shul* together. But one Sunday morning he opened a conversation that confirmed my increasing suspicion.

"I saw a show the other night, Belle," he said. "It posed an interesting dilemma."

"Oh?" I looked up from the dress I was embroidering for Ruth.

"Yes, well, it was a love triangle, see. There was the man, and his wife, who were happy enough. And then there was the lover, the fire that fueled the man's existence. Now, each woman offered attractive enticements: The wife was solid, steady, respectable. She performed all the requisite duties. She had interests of her own—community work, and so on. She was the mother of his child. Satisfactory, to be sure, but hardly what you'd call his passion.

"On the other hand, the lover was his heart's desire: A woman of adventurous spirit, a maverick who thrilled him, who touched his heart, but who may or may not prove to be acceptable. She made him feel the way he did when he was in a flying dream. Did you ever have a flying dream, Belle? It's like you're soaring free, yet safe from harm; physically and emotionally aloft, but serene.

"Anyway, the reason I was so interested in the play, the reason that I'm telling you about it now, is that it drew no ultimate conclusion. The playwright left the audience to decide which path the husband took.

"I wonder, Bella, which woman would you think he should choose?"

This was the question that Isaac raised time and again, over and over, in the most casual of conversations, never pressing the issue, really, though after a while it grated on me. What did I care for some fictional character in a play that I had never seen?

Yet still, he kept at me. Which woman would the protagonist pick, and why? Would his decision prove to be worthy, or would it reveal a fatal flaw?

*

I found my mind wandering in our book discussion group, away from the work at hand and back to the play that Isaac had described. I read the papers, and magazines. I had not heard of such a play. Why was this scenario, and this dilemma, of such interest to my husband?

Each day as I served lunch to the children in the school cafeteria line–a volunteer job I enjoyed—my mind meandered back to Isaac's description of characters. I could see bits of myself in his depiction of the wife—a depiction of his own making, as far as I could tell. I had actually sought out the play he spoke of, but could find nothing like it on Broadway or off. This particular type of work was mindless enough—ladling hot soup into small plastic bowls, popping a roll on the side of the dish—so I had plenty of time to think.

I did not think about the man in the play. I thought about my husband. I thought about him complaining of his daily commute, yet taking several hours away from home each weekend, supposedly to make an extra trip across town because he had forgotten something or other. I thought of his late arrivals home and of the liquor on his breath. I thought of his mornings, when he said he was composing music: Yet I had not seen a finished piece since Ruth was born. I thought of the night my water broke, when Isaac, inexplicably, had fled.

And I thought of our sex life. After the baby, he had told me that I should take my time, that it was not that important to him. I wanted to believe him, but I knew the passion of this man: If his sexual need was not met at home, he was probably getting it met somewhere else.

I did not want to admit it, did not want to face the fact that I was not woman enough to fulfill my husband. All my efforts had been for naught. I simply was not good enough—not pretty enough, clever enough, kind enough. I withered inside. How could this be? More than betrayed, I felt that I had let Isaac down.

I stared my naiveté in the face, and admitted that I had no way to confirm my discovery: I dared not confront him; I knew not who she was.

How could I have known that she would save me the trouble?

*

One look at her and I knew who she was, knew what she had come for. And yet I wanted to hear her out.

"May I help you?" I asked when I opened the door.

"May I come in?" she asked me back.

I allowed her to pass, offered her some tea, invited my husband's lover to sit in our front room as if she were a welcome guest.

"I guess you know why I'm here," she said.

"No," I answered. "I am afraid I do not."

"I'm not going to give him up," she said.

"I am sorry," I said. "I am afraid I do not know what you are talking about." False sincerity seeped from all sides.

She got blunt.

"I mean Ike," she said, pointedly. "I mean that I don't intend for him to stay."

"To stay?" I tried my best to feign innocence, ignorance.

"In this marriage. With you," she said. "I mean, Ike and I, we love each other, and, and, I don't intend for him to stay here much longer."

"*You* don't intend?" I asked, surprised.

"No, I don't," she answered, curtly. "I intend for him to be with me. That's what he wants, and me, too."

I blistered inside, and her words stung the seeping wound on my soul like iodine rubbed on a bloody cut. I cringed, I ached just to look at this woman—short, busty and brassy—telling me her intentions for my husband, and knowing, as well as I knew my own name, knowing deep in my soul that he loved her, and not me. But why? She was hardly remarkable: She was pushy, not pretty, not pleasant, not polished.

Just then, Ruth awoke from her nap.

"Your baby's crying," she stated the obvious.

"You had better go," I said.

*

I had a child. I had a home. I had a place in society that I was not willing to give up.

Paramour or no, Isaac had an obligation to me, to our child, to our home, to a life in which I played a prominent part. His lover could not intimidate me. I wondered whether he knew she had come. I wondered whether it was my place to say.

But of course it was.

A confrontation would allow me to state, in terms that even Isaac could not misinterpret, that I was no weakling, that I would not drift away like a feather whisked aside in a wisp of wind.

"Isaac," I said, one night after dinner. "Your Amalia came calling the other day."

He looked up but he did not speak.

"I want you to tell her not to return," I said.

Still nothing but a look from Isaac.

"You must stop seeing her immediately," I went on. "After all, I am in no position to give you up. We have a marriage. We have a home. We have a beautiful little girl.

"We have a good life, Isaac, a place in the community. Our families have long standing here. It would be foolish for you to sacrifice all that you are, all that you have achieved, on a sexual whim.

"Now, I know it will not be easy for you to make a break. You are not one who takes easily to rejecting others. I have thought this over carefully, and I think the best thing to do is to get away for a year or two, to allow Amalia the time to find someone else, and to recommit ourselves to each other. I am willing to forgive this embarrassment, Isaac, so long as you get rid of her now."

Isaac said nothing, still, so I assumed that he heard, appreciated and agreed with my words.

I assumed it was safe to forget Amalia's visit.

AMALIA

I don't know where I got the nerve.

I suppose I simply lost my patience, always waiting, hoping, but for what? For an event that I could not foresee. Only her death would make Ike free, and I hated myself for wishing death on someone I only knew second-hand. In truth, I probably would have liked her if I'd met her in some other way. We certainly shared a mutual interest. As it was, I resented her, ridiculed her, belittled her. She thought she was leading a respectable life, and she held her head up high with pride, but I knew the truth: That she could not satisfy her man.

The irony, of course, was that *I* was living the lie, that even though he loved me best, *I* was the secret, the cheat, the one lacking dignity. I had traded my honor in the name of love, but what had I to show for it?

I began to hate myself for what I'd become.

I became obsessively scrupulous, evading even the slightest hint of taint. I abandoned white lies. I lectured my nieces and nephews to do the right thing, to try to leave things better than they'd found them, to follow their hearts in pursuit of goodness.

Yet where had following my heart led me?

One gaping flaw rendered me a fraud.

*

How could I forfeit my life's love? Even the thought of ending our affair set my stomach to churning. He was the best thing that had ever happened to me. Was his towing the line such a terrible flaw? He blindly accepted his obligation. He could not conceive of a life-changing risk, could not imagine starting over again. And, disappointed though I was to hear him say so for himself, I could not change the fact that I loved him.

His loyalty was one of the qualities I admired most. That it worked to my disadvantage hardly seemed reason enough to dismiss it. So I added another wish to my list: That someday, his loyalty, like his love, would be mine.

*

That was before I missed my period. Once it was clear that I was bearing a child, *our* child, it seemed to me that my claim to Ike was just as legitimate as Bella's. Yes, they had a child to consider, but now, we would have a child, too. And frankly, I was losing my patience. Why did I have to be so understanding, so accommodating of a marriage that never should have occurred in the first place? My pride prevented me from using my pregnancy to force Ike into leaving her for me. I wanted him to *choose* me—for me, for love, and for himself, because he, too, deserved happiness. I did not want to present him with yet another burden to bear. So I made a promise to myself—to keep my condition confidential for as long as I could disguise it.

*

I joked with Ike before I went to Bella.

One morning after making love, lying naked in his arms, I asked if he wouldn't like to be with me always.

"That's my dream, my intention, my heart's desire," he said.

"Well, maybe I ought to pay Bella a visit, tell her how we feel, and see what she does. Maybe she'll throw you out: Problem solved." I smiled as I said it. He knew I was kidding.

But later, after we'd dressed and gone our separate ways for the day, I got to thinking: Well, why not?

I took a drink before I went, a shot of bourbon to boost my bravado. Ike taught Hebrew school in the afternoons. Bella and I would not be interrupted.

*

My heart was pounding when I approached their door. I took a swig from the flask I had brought along before I knocked.

I knew her face. It haunted me. But I doubted that she would recognize mine. Still, she must have suspected Ike. So much of his time was unaccounted for. And she knew what was missing from their married life.

She invited me into the home they shared, and I was struck by how little of Ike I felt there. The decor was all hers, or maybe her mother's. Heavy furniture upholstered in brocades, dark paneled walls, and hard-wood floors scattered with imported rugs. It was so formal that it intimidated me. This place was overbearing, severe. None of Ike's warmth or whimsy was here. Only the piano in the corner suggested that this might possibly be his place, too.

She treated me like she had invited me there. She even offered me a cup of tea. I guess she didn't know who I was, didn't know what I had come for. Or did she?

She certainly didn't make it easy. She made me spell it all out—that I wanted him, that he wanted me, that she should gracefully give him up. And although I thought I was being clear, she made me reiterate every word, as if she didn't quite comprehend. But she must have.

It was a good thing that I was drunk. Otherwise I never could have done it. Lucky for me, there was a baby in the house, because just when I thought I would die of discomfort the baby cried and Bella threw me out.

*

Afterward, Ike was angry with me.

"We're going to have to be very careful," he said. "She's forbidden me to see you any more. She'll be tallying up my time away, accounting for my every move. She wasn't even suspicious until you told her about us. Now every time I head toward the door, she asks me where I'm going and when I'll be back. What could you have been thinking, Mal?"

"I guess I thought that if she knew, that she might willingly step aside," I said. "*I* wouldn't want to live a lie. I guess it was just wishful thinking.

"Are you going to comply with her order not to see me?"

"Oh, Mal, I could never leave you again," his tone melted into softness. "Never. But we're going to have to be very cautious. We cannot flaunt ourselves in her face. The woman deserves her dignity. After all, she's the victim in all of this."

She's the victim? *She's* the victim? She's got the husband, the home, the legitimate lifestyle, and he thinks that *she's* the victim? I nearly lost my temper, but decided a tantrum would serve no good purpose, especially after the damage I had already done. "Mal," he said. "Amalia. My leaving her would mean my leaving here. If I fail to fulfill my family duties, I will be ostracized from the community. Our time together would be over. Our lives as we know them would be over. Even if it's not all that we want, let's not throw away all that we have."

BELLA

I knew I was pregnant again by the taste.

This time, there was every reason to tell him: To increase his obligation, to keep his attention focused at home, to elicit the kindness that he had shown me before.

After I confronted him with my knowledge of his affair, Isaac started making love to me. We had *Shabbos* again. And on the occasions I could muster the daring to show my own willingness to him, he obliged me during the week, as well. I would bathe in the evening with fragrant soaps, put up my hair and put on a thin nightgown. I would wait up until he got home from work, slip into bed and call to him from the bedroom. I smiled at him. I wanted to please him, to satisfy all of his needs at home. I did not exactly know what to do. There were no repositories for such information. But Isaac made it easy for me. He dutifully accepted all my invitations to bed.

So it hardly came as a big surprise that, after a few months of lovemaking at least a couple of times each week, that I conceived another child.

Still, my biggest advantage over Amalia was Ruth. Ruth was the apple of her father's eye. He doted on her: Read to her, sang to her, took her on walks. They were everything that fathers and daughters should be. They kept secrets, they giggled, they shared ice cream cones.

He imbued her with dreams for her happy future: A loving husband was sure to be hers, a family, homemaking abilities—especially cooking, baking, sewing and entertaining. He painted quite a picture of the way things ought to be, and I confess that I listened and tried to recreate his vision in our own home.

The love between the two of them was my insurance against infidelity: As long as I held Ruth's love, I knew that I held the key to Isaac's, too.

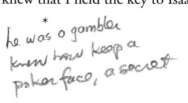

*

he was a gambler
knew how keep a
poker face, a secret

My pregnancy was difficult, made no less so by caring for Ruth. She was such an active three-year-old, curiously exploring all in her view. She stuck her fingers in every hole she could find, and, it seemed, immediately afterward, stuck them in her mouth. When I was not chasing after her, calling "no-no" as I went, I was busy wiping up the latest spill or scrubbing clean her face and hands.

She babbled endlessly, naming the objects she recognized, inquiring, "What's that?" of the ones she did not, and stringing words together into phrases and sentences that often directed our conversation.

She was full of rewards. Her fresh observations and perspectives never failed to bring a smile to my face. I had lost my wonder as I matured, as I lost my innocence. Ruth brought back a sense of marvel, a new view of the world. She rejuvenated my mind even as she exhausted my body, and I clung to her. She was my salvation.

The first few months of my second pregnancy I was so tired, yet I hardly got the chance to rest. Isaac paid little attention to me. We had been through it all before, though the first one was easier, and more exciting, simply because it was the first. This time he kept to his routine. He did not dote on me. But he did not place undue demands on me, either.

We seemed to reach a truce between us: We hardly discussed the tensions, though I felt them. The passion was fabricated from the start: I needed to believe I could meet his needs, and he was obliged to let me believe that I did. But now that we had an excuse to stop, we discontinued our love life again, with a degree of relief on both our parts.

I never again heard from Amalia, though I ached, both with curiosity and fear: Curiosity, on my good days, about what he had told her and how she had reacted; fear, when insecurity plagued me, that their romance continued, that he had paid me no heed, that Isaac and Amalia still were a pair.

Again and again, I raised the prospect of leaving New York for a year or two, of making a fresh start as a family of four. Most of the time, Isaac dismissed my suggestion, explained that his work, his family, his community were here. Anywhere else, we would be strangers. It made no sense to him to leave.

"We'll make our own fresh start right here," he placated me.

But still, I kept on, suggesting a sabbatical, suggesting that a change of setting would do us good.

And finally, in a weak moment, he relented.

"All right," he said. "I'll look into it."

AMALIA

At thirteen weeks I began spotting. The first spot was only the size of a quarter, but I knew that I wasn't supposed to be bleeding at all. I had missed two periods already. Now, three months later, I shouldn't start one. The fact that I'd heard of spotting heartened me. It was probably nothing to worry about. Still, I decided to see a doctor.

After my examination the doctor gave me the good news: That my cervix was closed, that there was no sign of dilation. But he gave me some bad news at the same time: That there was no apparent sign of life within me: No discernible fetal heartbeat and no indicator in my own slow pulse.

This, I couldn't understand. My breasts were tender and enlarged, my monthly period had stopped. I had all the common symptoms of pregnancy: Morning sickness and exhaustion and a taste for nothing at all, except bread. I felt dizzy, queasy throughout the day and my head spun when I lay down at night.

"Whatever you're feeling, and whatever the blood was, we won't be able to change the outcome," the doctor said, coldly, clinically. He looked down at my hands with, it seemed to me, some consternation for my lack of a ring. "You may abort yet; or you may not spot again. Whatever happens, it's in God's hands. There's nothing we can do to prevent miscarriage. If you want this child, my advice would be to take it easy, to keep your feet up for a day or two, and to see how you're feeling after that."

If I want this child?

I wanted this child.

So much for modern medicine.

*

I didn't last a day or two. I went home and climbed into my bed, and within two hours I began to cramp. It was what I imagined labor must be like. A long, hard contraction followed by a respite from pain, followed by another deep cramp that left my muscles tensed and my breath held tight until the bitter moment passed.

I was frightened and alone, and I had no one to call for help. I ran to the bathroom, desperately trying to squeeze my insides back in me, and failing—miserably, dropping them all over the floor—clumps of tissue and clots of blood that looked like raw turkey livers and giblets; deep red, solid masses swimming in borscht.

And the pain.

I cannot now distinguish the physical suffering from the emotional distress. I know that I hurt—deep in my womb and deep in my heart. I lay on the floor beside my mess, stunned still by the bloody remnants.

I had to clean it up myself, couldn't call for help, for no one else knew, and how could I tell, now that it was over? had to swab the thick puddle from the floor, rinse the rich, red blood in cold, cold water I drew from the tub, hoping, praying it wouldn't stain my sister's towel, eliciting questions I was too shattered to answer; had to gather up the solid pieces I imagined as bits of heart and bits of brain and pieces of my baby's soul, scoop them up and plunk them—gently, ever so gently, and lovingly—into the toilet, and flush them away as if they were nothing, and all the while some detached part of me, numbed with shock, could only hope that the bits of our baby wouldn't clog the plumbing.

What followed that dramatic episode was tedious by comparison: The longest, most painful menstruation I have experienced before or since. I could not move from the bed for several days, and I told my family I had influenza so that I could stay, undisturbed, in my room for as long as I believed I could, credibly. I only managed to make my way up out of the fear of undesirable consequences. My motivation was simple: To keep my nieces from calling the family doctor, who might detect the truth of the matter.

I longed to tell Ike, to whom I told all, yet I dared not confess to the secret I'd kept, not when we swore nothing was secret between us. I needed to know that he loved me still, that even though I'd lost our child, carelessly, though unintentionally, dropped it in a puddle of blood on the bathroom floor, that he would stick by me, care for me, and ultimately, someday, live with me.

He recognized the sadness in my heart through my eyes.

"Honey, what's the matter?" he asked one night as we sipped scotch whiskey between poker games.

But I could not bring myself to respond.

"You know you can tell me, Mal," he cooed. "It's me." He lifted my chin till my eyes looked in his. "We've never kept anything from each other."

"Oh, Ike," I dismissed him, "it's just more of the same. I get so frustrated with our situation. I want you so much, I love you so much. You are the most brilliant man I know. So clever. So wonderful. And yet, here we are, sneaking scotch in a bar, living our separate lives, forced to pretend, for the most part, that we don't even know each other. Sometimes it bothers me more than others. I guess I just think too much."

"I believe in us," he whispered to me. He cupped his hand on top of mine. "Somehow, some way. I believe."

It was the first time I had lied to Ike. I prayed that it would be the last.

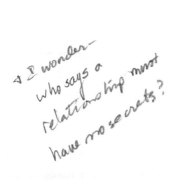

← I wonder—
who says a
relationship must
have no secrets?

BELLA

We named our boy David, after the boy in the Bible—faithful and strong, a leader, indeed, a savior of the Jewish people.

Isaac was thrilled to have a son to carry on the Grossman name. Nothing meant more to him than continuity, keeping intact the chain of tradition and advancing our people's destiny. Much as he loved Ruth, and there was no denying that, much as he loved little girl things—dress-ups and dolls and tea parties attended by imaginary friends—Isaac desperately had wanted a son. A girl would someday be promised away, would deliver children of someone else's name, who would carry on someone else's lineage. A boy, however, could sit right next to him in *shul*, could learn to lay *tefillin* and to recite the ancient morning prayer expressing thanks "for not creating me a woman." Of course he would never say so directly, but the fact of the matter was that a son was of paramount importance to Isaac. It was with great relief that I delivered him one.

From the very beginning, Isaac doted on David—ran to his crib when he cried out at night, carried him to me for nighttime feedings, took him on outings, on errands, to work, to show him off to his colleagues and friends. He concerned himself with the greatest details of David's care, even the matter of attire, choosing baby blue suits, baby booties and hats, and holding each piece up to the light to make sure that the fabrics and dye lots matched. He rocked the baby to sleep at naptime and was the first to his side when he awoke.

It was a love story, to be sure, and if the children were the stars, I was content to have a supporting role. My world seemed stable, even secure, and for that I was immensely grateful. We were a well-oiled, fully functional family, partaking in our community—participating in Hebrew school functions and synagogue activities and mixing with other families like ours. We were secure financially. My parents provided a great deal of support as their *tallis* business prospered and grew. We had moved to a larger apartment just before David was born, with enough bedrooms for us each to have our own, plus a study for Isaac, and a large kitchen for me, and a living room and separate dining room. I wanted for nothing of consequence. And I focused my world on my happy family.

*

With things between us smooth and secure, I wanted to widen our family circle. I began to invite relatives to dinner, to share festivals and holy days and our weekly *Shabbos* ritual. It was good for the children to learn the *mitzvah* of hospitality; it was good to show them they were part of a greater whole, a community of family friends and relations; and it was good for me and Isaac to function socially, publicly, as a couple.

I started with my own people, because I was most comfortable with them. My parents became regulars at our table, and sometimes stayed with the children while we took an after dinner stroll, or attended a community or social function.

Both Ruth and David took to their grandparents, who doted on them without restraint. They were not my parents' only grandchildren, but, perhaps because of the strife I had subtly hinted my marriage had withstood, my mother, especially, wanted to do all that she could to support my relationship with Isaac. We had no shortage of money, thanks to my family. In addition, my mother offered her time—time with the children so Isaac and I could have time to ourselves, time helping me with the children in the evening after Isaac had gone to the cinema, time running the errands we lacked the time to attend to. Sometimes she even loaned us her maid.

My sisters and their families, too, came around. We hosted the family *Chanukah* party. What fun! Children ranging in age from one to twelve, all dancing wildly, singing songs, eating *latkes* and opening gifts. They gambled with the *gelt* we gave them—using the chocolate coins wrapped in gold foil as chips in the lively, betting game of *dreidl*. The older children looked after the young ones, freeing the adults to mix, undistracted, after we lit the *chanukiyahs*.

I relished the family times we shared, and savored the chance to be with my sisters again, to huddle in the kitchen and whisper family secrets—giggling over which of the cousins had a crush on the other, boasting of each of our husbands' professional stature, confessing to wishes of new houses in suburbs, and debating who had had the latest run-in with Pop. We laughed, and in our merriment, the years living apart, in our separate homes, melted away like so much *schmaltz* in a pot of chicken soup. It was good to feel the warmth of their embraces, the heat of their hearts in my already warm kitchen, and I felt contentment with my lot.

Isaac enjoyed the family times, too, but missed his brothers' jocularity. The Grossmans had a particular, and peculiar, sense of humor, appreciating, and embellishing each other's homespun jokes, which none but them found to be funny.

One of Isaac's favorites was one that I found inane: "Can you say fish without moving your lips?" he would ask, a smirk already springing to his smile. He would hardly give his listener time to digest the question, when he was spilling the answer, "Herring."

Anyway, after a few fun, but tame times with my parents, my sisters and brothers, their spouses, and their children, Isaac suggested including his clan. I was only too happy to oblige, and offered to make a dinner for both sides of the family.

In addition to his brothers, Isaac invited a young Dr. Grant, his first cousin once removed, raised in Toronto, who had set up a medical practice in New York. Dr. Grant was slightly younger than we were, and single. His grandfather and Isaac's father were brothers. After he finished medical school, he changed his name from Grossman to Grant, not to shun the Jewish community, but to make his practice more palatable to gentile patients as well as Jews. He hardly hid his identity; in fact, many of his gentile patients had sought him out *because* he was Jewish.

He was a psychiatrist, an interesting field in interesting times, or so he told us over dinner. Never had his profession received so much attention since the popular press had taken hold of the work of the famous Dr. Freud, whom he had had the privilege of meeting at one of his fancy conferences.

Dr. Grant fit in with the Grossmans as if he had grown up with them. He laughed at their jokes and added to them; his expressions and gestures mimicked theirs. He was comfortable with himself, and that made us comfortable with him, too.

I liked Dr. Grant—I called him Dr. Grant because that is what he called himself and Isaac had not mentioned his first name to me. I liked his short, well-groomed goatee, his brown, wavy hair combed back in a pompadour, the lyrical lilt of his speaking voice, his tweed coat, pleated pants and skinny neck tie. He was the first man who had ever cleared his own plate from my table: He did not offer to do it, he just stood up and carried it out to the kitchen. No fuss and no muss. Just a matter of course. Our Dr. Grant was quite a *mensch*, and he became a fixture at our table.

Isaac liked him, too. Often, after a meal, they would retreat to the den, to light up cigars and talk man-to-man. I did not feel excluded, mind you. I was so happy to have Isaac at home, ensconced in engaging, yet harmless, conversation. They sometimes spent hours behind closed doors. For all I know, Dr. Grant was shrinking Isaac's head, but they would come out laughing, Isaac slapping him on the back. So I quickly dismissed any thoughts of manipulation, and assumed that they simply enjoyed one another's company.

Some evenings, when Isaac was at the cinema and after I had tucked the children in bed, Dr. Grant would come by for coffee and cake. He was exceptionally good company, always up on current affairs, and on the latest medical trends. Sometimes, as the evening wore on, we would delve more into our personal lives. As I said, I found him quite attractive, although a bit on the prim side of neat. His long, delicate fingers reminded me of Isaac's, though Dr. Grant had no musical leanings:

Neither keys nor strings were graced by his touch. Still, he lifted his cup with refined elegance, and transported sweets from the plate to his lips with a simple grace.

I commented on his easy style—not only his manners, but the ease with which he melded into Isaac's family, without much childhood experience with them. I contrasted him to the men I knew. For example, both my father and Isaac approached a table with a sense of purpose: They aimed to move food efficiently from plate to palate; they were unconcerned, perhaps unaware, of the social amenities that a dinner could provide its company.

Perhaps I revealed more about myself and my biases than I should have, for our conversation led him to ask a question I thought he knew the answer to.

"Your social behaviors do contrast so," he noted. "How, by the way, did you and Isaac meet?"

"We met at our wedding," I answered. I must have looked surprised, because he did. Already, just half a dozen years after we had wed, arranged marriages were falling out of favor, and more and more couples—even from the most traditional families—were finding love matches for themselves, through courtships that led, ultimately, to marriages of their own making. I was happy, for my children's sake. It made more sense. It allowed a thoughtful person to make a reasoned choice. It allowed a girl to be swept off her feet.

"And, would you, Bella, like to be swept off your feet?" Dr. Grant probed.

"I suppose I never thought of it," I answered. "For as long as I can remember, I knew that I had been promised to Isaac, so I never thought about finding romance, or falling in love. My focus was always on home-making, child rearing, pleasing my husband."

"And do you?" he asked.

"Do I what?"

"Please your husband."

"I suppose I do," I answered curtly, wishing now, that Isaac would get home, wishing that the specter of Amalia would leave my consciousness.

"I'm sorry. I didn't mean to pry. I guess I forgot to leave my profession at the office.

"Gee, this cake is delicious, Bella. Did you bake it yourself?"

"No," I said, with flat expression. "I did not. It came from the bakery down the street."

"Honestly, I'm sorry. Maybe I'd better go."

"Maybe that would be best," I said, with a perfunctory nod.

*

I got to wondering about how much Dr. Grant knew of my family, my marriage. He had crossed my line of privacy, and I had let him know it. But I wondered what he had pieced together from hours of conversation with Isaac, many of them lubricated with dinner wine and after-dinner *schnapps*. I wondered where Isaac drew his line and what he may have disclosed, even if inadvertently.

I began to feel uncomfortable around Dr. Grant, not for any change in his demeanor, but because I suspected he knew more about me than I wished him to know. On the surface, he was as charming as ever, quick with a compliment or a helpful hand. He gazed on me with appropriate affection, he still cajoled with the best of the Grossmans, and was always at the top of Isaac's guest list, right behind the Grossman brothers. I had no reason to think that our run-in had registered permanently, but I had to get over my discomfort; not only was Dr. Grant our relative, but now, it developed, he was Isaac's friend. Since Isaac and I had begun to enjoy and make a practice of family entertaining, he would be a presence in our home, whether I liked it or not, and I preferred to resolve to like it.

Let bygones be bygones, I told myself. He is like a child who needed to test my limit; I drew the line. Nothing more complicated than that. He had not invaded my privacy since; I had no reason to believe that he would again.

I decided to make amends, and Dr. Grant made it easy for me.

It was *Shabbos*. We had eaten well. We were relaxed. Isaac went to kiss the children good-night, and Dr. Grant helped me with the dishes.

"Dr. Grant," I began.

"Don't you think it's about time you started calling me Joshua?" he gently interrupted.

We stood, hip to hip, at the kitchen sink. I rinsed and washed; he dried and stacked.

"Joshua," I said. "Joshua, you must forgive my sense of propriety. I grew up in a traditional home, with little latitude for original thought, let alone wishes, dreams, or heart's desires. There were tight proscriptions on my behavior and I learned early on not to question authority. I was told what my lot in life would be; I accepted it, plain and simple.

"But now, as an adult, I see there are other ways, new ways, some of them better ways. And I am grateful. For my children's sake, mostly, but for my own, too. The other night you challenged me, and I was unprepared. I am afraid I reacted like the little girl who does what she is told, whose fate is sealed and whose life is unexamined. I suspect there was more than a speck of truth in your line of questioning, or I would not have displayed such an inhospitable reaction. I would like it very much if we could forget that conversation, and continue our friendship, our kinship, as if it had not taken place."

"Consider it done," Joshua said glibly. "I probably overstepped the line of common decency, anyway."

I turned to peck him on the cheek as a gesture of forgiveness and goodwill, but even as I did so, doubt cast a shadow over my kiss.

*

One day, in the street market, I overheard gossip: That coquettish Amalia Abramowitz was recovering from a miscarriage. She had gotten herself pregnant and—see, there is a just God, they said—He had done away with the child she bore, which certainly must have been unwanted.

Ah, what some people will say to diminish the downtrodden! Now that things between Isaac and me were stable, I was actually able to muster some pity for Amalia. After all, the poor girl was terribly plain, she had no dowry, no money, no hope for a future even remotely resembling the life that the girls of my social caste dreamed of, and expected. She had squandered any semblance of reputation: Everyone knew about her and Isaac, though no one that I knew had the lack of good taste to mention their affair to me.

She must have taken up with someone else, I thought, quick to believe the rumor mill. Or had she? Doubt still nagged me.

What if the baby she lost was Isaac's?

Now that our children were beyond babyhood, and my life had settled into a predictable rhythm, getting away from here, and from *her*, took top priority on my list.

                                    *

Dr. Grant became my ally, or so I thought. Now that we had made our peace, we spent more and more time together, just the two of us. He never brought any friends around. He seemed to have no social life. Rather, his life revolved around his practice and us, his newfound family. He spent at least an evening a week at our house, chatting with me over cookies and tea while Isaac was still at work. Then, when Isaac came home, the two of them often stayed up well into the morning hours, while I excused myself to bed. Weekends we often entertained, and Dr. Grant was always happy to lend me a helping hand in the kitchen: Arranging platters, filling glasses, cleaning dishes after the meal.

(Even though he had asked me to call him by his first name, and I felt no residual resentment toward him, I still preferred to address him by the more formal, "Dr. Grant." It demonstrated both my respect and my distance. Although he was *mishpochah*, I did not want to risk his becoming overly familiar again.)

He told me about his upbringing. He had had a strong, and sometimes domineering mother who made all the decisions for the household. His father was quiet, even withdrawn. Dr. Grant was the oldest child in his family; he had three younger sisters. Often, and much to his dismay, his mother would dress all four children alike. Although he protested, she made it clear that he had no choice in what he wore. To me, now, her imposition of will—at least in the area of his attire—seemed to have done him no permanent harm: He dressed impeccably, if scholarly, just as Isaac did.

He was educated in a *yeshiva* from kindergarten through grade twelve. Upon reaching adolescence, he rebelled against the system, wearing his hair a little too long; sometimes refusing to wear a *kippah*. He studied not religion, as he was instructed to, but thought: He took a progressive path—from Judaism to theology, and later to philosophy and psychology, which led him, ultimately to psychiatry. He wondered about the inner workings of the mind—not only his own, but his mother's, his sisters', and particularly his father's. What forces precipitated a man's divorcing himself from his own life, he wondered?

Though he had had to study anatomy, biology and the like—first, to earn admission to medical school, and, once in, to pass his examinations—he took little interest in things physical. In fact, he struck me as rather squeamish. One year, at *Pesach*, the children were running, wildly, after the meal, after receiving bags of candy as their reward for finding the hidden *afikomen*. One of my sister's boys, a four-year-old, tripped and fell, gashing his eyelid against the sharp corner of the cedar chest at the foot of Ruth's bed. Blood spurted everywhere, or so it seemed. The child wailed—less from pain than from fear at the sight of his own blood—and none of us in the house knew quite what to do. We rushed about, some of us gathering ice and towels while others encircled the boy in an effort to offer comfort to him. The child did not stop gushing blood, and finally had to be taken to a hospital.

Later, we wondered, first, each of us to ourselves, and then, reluctantly, aloud to one another, what had become of Dr. Grant? As a practicing, licensed psychiatrist, he had been through four years of medical school. Yet in our medical emergency, in the hubbub of the accident, he had slinked off, quietly, evading the mania, dodging the mess.

Other behaviors led me to believe he was finicky, too. Well, perhaps that is too harsh. But he was precise. His manner was delicate; he listened intently. His voice was rich and smooth, his words well-crafted, and well-selected. It was calming just to hear him speak. His intonation was lyrical. His step was light; he all but skated when he made his way back to the den with Isaac.

To Isaac, Dr. Grant provided the excuse to drink. Isaac always made sure there was liquor aplenty the nights that he knew Dr. Grant was coming, and they would often finish a fifth between them, either of vodka, or of peppermint *schnapps,* or of a heavy-bodied, fruity brandy, the type that always made me sick. Once Dr. Grant's practice of dropping by became regular, Isaac for the first time routinely kept liquor in the house. Now, even if Dr. Grant was not with us, the liquor was. Isaac drank it with gusto, with two alternating results: He either became boisterous—loose-lipped, loud, bordering on obnoxious—or he became horribly cantankerous, so much so that I had to shield the children from his mean-spirited bark, most often directed not at them, but at me.

Sometimes, we discussed it, Dr. Grant, and I, and I thought that he might say something to Isaac, something of a professional nature that would lead Isaac to see that his drinking behavior was not serving him well.

Instead, it seemed to me that, though I knew not why, Dr. Grant encouraged him. But why not? When Isaac was boisterous, he was plenty of fun—at least, I thought a man would find him fun. When Isaac was nasty, Dr. Grant simply left.

I implored Dr. Grant to help me with Isaac.

"Don't you see how the liquor affects him?" I asked.

"He goes out of his way to get it in the house. When he drinks in the evening, he becomes anti-social. He cannot play with the children; he cannot talk with me. By morning, he is weak and sick from overindulgence, and his creative time is lost to a series of antacids and analgesics that prop him up enough to get through the rest of the day."

"Could be worse," Dr. Grant remarked. "At least you know where he is when he's drinking. You don't have to worry about infidelity. And after all, if that's his only vice…"

"But it's not," I said. "Have I not told you about the gambling?"

"Ike gambles?" he asked.

"Whenever he gets the chance," I said.

"Interesting," was all that he said in response.

*

Our love life was as lively as it ever had been. No fireworks, to be sure, but pleasant and comfortable, and frequent enough. Still, I could not shake the nagging worry that Isaac was straying from home again.

The children were the glue that bound our family together. How he loved them! As David grew out of infancy, through toddlerhood into young boyhood, Isaac took him uptown to outfit him in miniature versions of his own apparel from the waist up, and matching knickerbockers below. In his bow ties and tam o'shanters, David was quite a dapper lad.

I was responsible for Ruth's clothes, taking great pains to sew beautiful dresses, putting my millinery trade school education to work by creating matching hats for her every outfit. Her schooling, though, was Isaac's concern. She attended Hebrew school now, and commuted back and forth with her father. They sometimes diverted from the straight course, detouring to adventures she would share over dinner. And always, Isaac would pipe up with an embellishment or two. He could hardly help himself from *kvelling*. He found her witty, talented and adorable. What more could a father want from a daughter?

At Hebrew school, he would visit her class to offer a few words of encouragement to the children—he was Director of Hebrew Instruction now. Then he would summon her into the hall. Wide-eyed, like a child unveiling pilfered cookies to a special pal, he would extend his palm to offer her a candy drop or a stick of chewing gum. "Now, don't tell the others where that came from," he would tell her, as if the other children would not know when Ruth returned with a fistful of sweets.

She loved telling tales of Poppy's pocketful of candy when she got home from school in the evening. I was supposed to act surprised. I would wink at Isaac and feign disbelief—a ritual that ended in a raft of giggles.

He maintained his routine of spending large chunks of time away from home, but I was so busy tending our growing family that I hardly concerned myself with that. He was industrious, enterprising. His talents were in such demand and his energy level so high that much of the time he was working two and three different jobs, staging children's plays at the Hebrew Educational Society in Brooklyn, leading choirs at the Educational Alliance on the Lower East Side, preparing boys for *bar mitzvah* at the Kane Street Synagogue. What mattered to me was that our times together were happy, engaging, enriching. Our children knew that they were loved, and for my part, I knew that I was, too.

Yet, I found myself plagued, still, by the thought of Amalia. I could sense her lurking in the distance, plotting "chance meetings" that Isaac would not, could not resist. So long as Isaac was accessible, Amalia would not cast her sights on another. And, to be truthful, I was unsure of Isaac's ability, or interest, in rebuffing her advances. Her interest in my man was fierce. And the more I thought about it, the more I knew that my marriage would not be totally stable until Amalia had found herself a man of her own. I had to give her the chance to do that. I had to remove Isaac from her grasp for long enough that she would take up with someone else.

I refocused on going away for a while, perhaps as long as a year or two, to explore, to recommit ourselves to each other, to get away from Amalia.

*

"Isaac," I said.

He looked up from his paper.

I sat on the hassock next to his armchair and held my open hands out to him.

"Isaac, my darling." I began. "I have been thinking and thinking of how to break out of my rut…"

"It's been hard on you, Dear," he responded kindly. "The babies weren't easy. *I* wasn't easy. But we're back on track now. The children are older. Everything will be all right."

He patted my hands to comfort me and began to turn back to his reading.

"No, Isaac, it is more than that," I said. "I need a change of scenery, a place to get away to, just us, just the four of us, for a while."

"A vacation?" Isaac said. "But, of course. What a splendid idea!"

"No, no, I do not mean a vacation. I mean more time than that. A lot more time. Like a sabbatical, Isaac. Like for a year or two."

"A year or two? I thought you had put that craziness behind you, Bella. Our life is here, our families, our friends, Ruth's school, my work…"

He paused.

"How on earth could we leave for that length of time?"

"Other communities need educators. Other communities might like to stage plays. We could try, could we not? We could look. It would be good for the children to see more of their country than just the City of New York. And I would welcome the respite, Isaac. I need a break, really and truly, I do."

"Bella, Bella," he patted my hands and looked at me with regret.

"Isaac?" I looked back at him, hopefully.

"Well, I'll nose around," he turned back to his paper. "We'll see, all right?"

"All right," I said.

The seed was planted.

*

A few nights later, I raised the subject again, over dinner.

"Isaac," I said. "Have you thought any more about going away?"

"Hmmmm?" He seemed not to recall our earlier discussion.

"You remember. The change of scenery? The opportunity to see more of our country? The family adventure?"

"Are we going on a trip?" Ruth piped up.

"Maybe, Honey," I answered brightly.

David looked at Isaac, and then at me, wondering what we were talking about.

"Poppy and I were talking about moving to another place for a while, to see how people in other places live," I said. "And I just wondered whether he had thought any more about where we should go, maybe someplace out west, or down south? And I was wondering how long before we might be able to leave?"

Ruth beamed an "oh boy!" sort of smile at her father, and David followed suit as any younger brother would.

"Really, Poppy?" Ruth asked, excitement making her voice pitch rise. "Golly, the Wild West! Wouldn't that be something! I'll bet Cousin Miriam would be jealous!"

If there was anything that Isaac hated to do, it was to disappoint the children. The moment that Ruth expressed enthusiasm for the idea, I knew that I was that much closer.

"Well, now, let's really think about this," Isaac turned to Ruth. "It would mean a new school, new teachers, new friends, and no more family gatherings. You wouldn't see Cousin Miriam for a very long time."

"But I want to go, Poppy! Really, I do! Can we? Can we?"

"Well, I'll have to look into this further," Isaac said.

I was yet another step closer, or further, as it were, from Amalia.

AMALIA

"I can't see any way around it, Mal. She keeps bringing it up. Now the children are in on it. They're all excited. I'm afraid I'm going to have to go."

We were dressing in my friend Sadie's apartment, preparing to say our good-byes for the day. Sadie was a good one. As long as she was gone to work she was happy to leave a key under the doormat for us. She understood our situation. A part of her, at least, sympathized with its impossibility.

"I can't stand this. Really. Can't you just tell her 'no' and be done with it?" I hitched my stocking up over my thigh.

"Mal, we've been through that over and over again. It's not her. It has very little to do with her. You know I love you more, and in every way possible." He ogled me, rather amorously for someone who'd only just finished taking me, but then forced himself to look away. "But there are other considerations. The children, for one."

"So, you're going to go, just like that?"

"Not 'just like that.' And, before you get too angry, I have to tell you, I have a plan."

"Oh, well then. A plan." I rolled my eyes heavenward, wondering what on earth he could be thinking.

"Where we go has been left to me to decide, based, I suppose, on work opportunities, and suitability for family life."

"So?"

"So, I've been asking around. I've been doing some reading. And I sent away for some literature. *The Reno Newsletter. 1924.* Listen to this," he reached into his satchel to retrieve a magazine. "'Reno is noted far and wide for its genial wholehearted spirit of hospitality.'

"And this: 'Reno is a city of organized women…Reno women are taking a great interest in organized child-welfare work.'

"And this: 'The Nevada Musical Club has stood out in a class by itself as of social and educational value for the past seven years in bringing to Reno the artists of the world.'

"They've got good schools, attractive housing, paved roads, movie theaters that need organists, they've got lakes and mountains we can take the children to visit, they've even got a small Jewish community..."

"Ike, why am I listening to all of this?" I was quite annoyed.

"Because, Mal, Reno is a divorcement city. Nevada has the most relaxed divorce laws in the country. Only a six-month waiting period, and no need to show either cause or fault. By establishing residency there, Bella and I will qualify for quick divorcement, which I will pursue at the appropriate time. And that, my Dear, will free me to marry you."

"Really, Ike?"

"Really." A tear welled up in his eye as he said it, as if saying so out loud made it done.

He pulled me toward him, slipping my camisole strap down my shoulder and slipping his hand down inside, to my skin.

We kissed, a long, slow kiss with bodies touching all the way down, from our mouths to our chests to our bellies to our thighs. Our legs were entwined. Even our feet were touching.

"Watching you dress makes me want you again," he whispered.

"Sounds like we've got something to celebrate," I answered.

I released my embrace around his neck to slide his still-unbuttoned shirt off his shoulders. His warm hand caressed my thigh. My garters weren't fastened yet. He ran his hand over the curve of my hip, up my side, lifting my camisole off as it went, over my head and then, cupping his hand around my back for support, he lowered me onto my back, down onto the rug.

One hand cupped my bottom, and long, thin fingers stretched to reach between my legs. The other gently stroked my breast, reigniting the passion consummated only moments earlier. I pulled away, but gently so. Could I allow myself another? I didn't want to peak without him.

"Ike?" I whispered, wondering.

"Go with it, Darling," he whispered back. "My greatest pleasure lies in pleasing you."

I threw back my head and arched my back, and let Ike take me where angels fly.

*

We dressed again, but hastily this time. We were late now, for our routine obligations. We had to hurry our conversation.

"In the meantime," Ike said, picking up where he left off, "I'm putting you under the care of my nephew, Dr. Joshua Grant. He'll take you out. He'll make a proper escort for you. He'll take you wherever you wish to go. You'll like him, Mal. Just don't like him too much. I want you to wait for me, after all."

"I can't believe you told someone about us," I was exasperated. "I thought we agreed, until the time came when we could be open about our relationship that we would keep it to ourselves."

"All I told him was that I knew a young woman he might enjoy socially. I certainly didn't kiss and tell all, Mal. And this way, you'll have a friend while I am away."

"I don't need a watch dog, Ike," I said. "Tell your nephew not to bother with me."

"But it's already been arranged. You'll meet him through the proper channels."

*

I "officially" met Joshua Grant through a "friend of a friend" who was making social introductions for him. He was a doctor, new to New York, single and eligible—in a *yenta's* words, a catch. I should be grateful for the introduction, for the opportunity to charm the charming Dr. Joshua Grant, and, perhaps, with luck, to turn his head, at least that's what my nieces said. I wasn't much interested in being tended while Ike was out of the state with his wife, but, the deal was set. I couldn't very well decline the opportunity without raising the aura of suspicion, though, of course I had no interest in him, or in anyone, but Ike.

But to my surprise, Joshua and I struck an almost instant rapport.

He was easy to talk to, to confide in. I suppose he selected the right field for himself. Who wouldn't be able to bare his soul, given enough time with this gentle man? He was kind and sensitive. He seemed to understand me. He had a quality much like Ike's—protective and caring, but without the dash of daring, the spark of excitement that could turn my fondness into fire.

It was hard for me to remain entirely uninterested since he was Ike's nephew, and so much like the Grossman clan. He was handsome, too, and bright, and well-off, all of which made it impossible to explain an immediate rejection. So as long as he asked me on a Sunday stroll, out to eat or to a show, I had no choice—with the whole neighborhood watching—but to agree to go out with him. Still, I remained aloof toward him, giving him no encouragement.

For his part, he did not press me, nor did he seem at all disappointed by my coolness. In fact, he almost seemed relieved, so much so that I wondered whether Ike really had told Joshua of our relationship before he left New York. I mean, it was more than a lack of expectation on his part. Joshua never *initiated*, not so much as a touch of my hand, not so much as a peck on my cheek. I'd never known a man not to try at least a little something, which led me to believe he knew the truth—that I was desperately in love with Ike.

*

"I must frustrate you," Joshua observed after several months.

"Why would you say that?" I asked.

"Well, you must know that I *like* you, Amalia. Otherwise, I wouldn't keep calling on you."

"Sure, and I like you, too, Joshua." I was about to pat his leg, but pulled back my hand before I touched him. After all, he had yet to touch me.

"But…?" he asked.

"But, what?"

"But you are surprised at the lack of, em, the lack of intimacy between us?"

"Well," I admitted. "To each his own."

"Yes, I thought so," he nodded, downcast.

"Thought what?" I said. I was confused.

"We both know." He was dejected. "It's a simple matter of preference, isn't it?"

"Did *he* tell you?" I was flustered and embarrassed, suspecting that Joshua had known all along about me and Ike.

"*He? Tell* me?" now he seemed perplexed. "Who? Did who tell me what?"

My heart sank into my stomach as I realized the truth: That Joshua had no prior knowledge of my love affair with Ike, only a speck of suspicion, and a speck of guilt, that propelled him to probe me.

"I'm sorry, Amalia. When I first met you I thought, I *hoped*, I really did, that you might be the one to change me, that you and I might make a nice couple, but…" He was unable to finish his sentence, just hunched his shoulders, stared into his hands and silently cried.

It was a long time before we pieced together that we each had confessed to our separate secrets: that I was waiting for Ike, and that he was homosexual. But once we'd struck a mutual allegiance, I knew that Joshua Grant would help my cause. After all, he, like me, valued living an honest life, at least as honest as he dared, and between us we figured we'd bring Ike around to choosing to follow his heart, just as we each had chosen to follow ours.

BELLA

The hustlers bustling around the station personified Reno's reputations. Cowboys, handsome and rugged, hauled high stacks of monogrammed bags to wagoneers awaiting them, while high-toned women marched behind—pointing here, gesturing there—directing them to add this bag or that to their already mountainous loads of luggage. Such women, stamped with the unmistakable mark of the East Coast-elite, were shipped West by wealthy spouses for solo vacations on the dude ranch, or, some, I imagined, sought out holidays *sans* husbands, the highlights of which were the cowboys themselves. Lawyers, dressed in three-piece suits with gold chains swinging from pin-striped watch pockets, flocked to meet forlorn-looking ladies who arrived alone to pursue forced divorces—divorces pre-arranged from a distance by too-busy, too-bored, or two-timing husbands. If I had not been so persistent in wanting to come here as a family, I fear I may have wound up here like them. Quickly, I surveyed the station's foot traffic, clutched for each of the children's hands, and alit from the train into the midday hub-bub. It was twelve o'clock noon.

"Looking for a divorce, Lady?" squawked a lawyer hawking his services in much the same way a newsboy might peddle the daily "Extra."

I looked away.

Quite the contrary, I was thinking to myself when I ran smack into ill-repute. Reno's red light district flaunted its wares: A golden nude decorated The Club Fortune marquee; Coldbrandt's front sign promised nude girls within. Instinctively, I covered the children's eyes with my palms. There was more: A turmoil of shack-stores and cheap saloons, tough alleys, and tatoo shops. The confusion of sights and lights befuddled me, even in daylight, and I hurried to hire a motor car that would carry us to our new home, though I held out little hope for this new town, based on my seamy first impression.

But as the taxi cab carried us west, through downtown and beyond, along the bank of the Truckee River, I saw an entirely different Reno. Downtown looked downright respectable. New motor cars angled neatly in front of a produce stand, a furniture store, a general store, the post office, the newspaper office, and on and on all down the main drag. Well-dressed men and women greeted each other on sidewalks, exchanging pleasantries and conversation. An orderly line of people awaited tickets at the movie theater box office, which had just opened for the matinee show. The street was well-swept: No litter marred the arterials, neither human—as it had, close to the station—nor otherwise. Further west, we passed green parks, sprawling lawns dotted with mallard ducks, fishermen casting lines off small boats nestled next to the river's bridge, a breathtaking view of the snow-capped Sierra, and well-maintained homes, both big and small.

Reno, it appeared, was a two-faced town, and far livelier than I would have imagined. It certainly would not have been my first choice, but I was happy to be out of New York, out of the clutches of that desperate woman. Out of sight, out of mind, I told myself, hoping against hope that this exodus would turn the tide, would cast Amalia's line in another direction, in any direction away from my husband.

Isaac had come a few weeks ahead of the children and me, had found us a furnished house to rent, a darling little clapboard place on a tree-lined street called Ralston Avenue. A wooden porch led the way to the front door, and a grassy patch out front invited Ruth and David to play outdoors nearly year round, as we would learn: The weather was temperate—neither too cold in the winter nor too hot in the summer. The furnishings were not my taste, rather western in style—roped piping on the sofa, for example, and a horsey motif on the armchair upholstery, and wood-covered floors, all in brown and rust tones—but the place was clean enough after I scrubbed it down, and comfortable enough, with separate bedrooms for each of the children and for us, and a bathroom with a tub, a flush toilet and hot and cold running water.

Isaac found work easily, stringing odd jobs together much the same as he had at home. The Majestic Theater downtown was eager to hire an organist, so much so that the manager outbid Isaac's first offer, from the Grand. Although there was no shortage of artistic types in town, few of the better pianists would stoop to accompanying the moving pictures. Most of them were wealthy socialites, here only temporarily, to establish residency so that they could divorce spouses left behind, in New York, in Washington, in Hollywood. While I did not approve of their motive, I was grateful for their presence here, for it lended a cosmopolitan air to an otherwise small town that managed to escape sheer provincialism only by being the biggest and most accessible spot in a largely unregulated state, situated, as it was, on the transcontinental railroad line. News from the most powerful circles on the Eastern Seaboard seemed to find its way straight to Reno, and to a New York girl like me, it was a welcome arrival.

The town's public schools were set up for stage shows, but few of the teachers knew how to direct, let alone how to direct children in the theater arts. Isaac quickly found parents eager to utilize the schools' well-appointed auditoria, most of which had seating capacities of up to five hundred, stages with drop-curtains, parlor and garden scenes, footlights and border lights, and suitable dressing rooms. The high school auditorium was even more grand: An upper gallery expanded seating capacity to nine hundred persons, a larger and more finely equipped stage than the four grade schools, and five sets of scenery. It took only a month or two for the schools to discover and capitalize on Isaac's penchant for children's musical theater.

As we settled in to our new lifestyle, we learned that a small Jewish congregation met Saturday mornings in the assembly hall at the Congregational Church. So grateful were the members of the *Chebra B'ris Shalom* Society, as it was known—bankers, lawyers, and local merchants, mostly—that they happily paid Isaac a tidy sum to provide music at the services, and Hebrew instruction for their children. They did not even have a rabbi. Until our arrival, few *bar mitzvahs* had taken place; no one in town was adept enough to train a boy to read *Torah*. And when a Jewish couple married here, they had to import a rabbi from San Francisco.

The congregants' levels of observance were varied. I was surprised to look across the room at the men. (The room was divided by men and women in the front, with mixed seating at the rear for the less observant.) Although these men chose to sit and pray separately from the women, many of them went without *tallisim*. It was unclear to Isaac and to me whether they had shed the tradition, or whether their own prayer shawls had worn thin, and there were no new ones available for sale in this town.

In any case, Isaac drew quite an amount of attention when he arrived wearing his fine, machine-stitched, silk *tallis* from New York. The men eyed him from their seats in the *shul*, and one older, rather bold gentleman even approached him at the *kiddush* lunch—the social mixer after the service.

"Such a fine *tallis*," he proclaimed to Isaac, pinching the fabric between his fingers.

"You like it?" Isaac asked, happy to make conversation.

I was proud of my family's fine workmanship. "I wonder," the man started, "whether you have another…"

"Another?" Isaac was startled. "Why, yes, of course. I have many." He winked at me. "Why do you ask?"

"Why? Well, young man, when I came west, a long, long time ago, I brought a single *tallis* with me. I wore it every *Shabbos,* every holy day, every morning as I said my prayers. The threads wore thin, but still, I wore it. Where would I buy another in Reno, heh? But finally, time took its eventual toll, and I had to bury the tattered cloth, so tattered that it could no longer be of use to me in my service to God."

"I see," Isaac grew solemn.

"I wonder, young man, whether you could loan me one of yours—not this very fine embroidered one, but perhaps, another one, a simple one, so that I might return to the traditional attire for prayer?"

Ceremoniously, Isaac unfurled his *tallis* and wrapped it around the gentleman's shoulders.

"May you wear it in peace, in strength, and in service to God," Isaac said quietly to this stranger.

And I wept, for I knew that he had brought just this one prayer shawl to Reno.

*

People moved in and out of here so quickly that liaisons were forged hastily, and without too many questions asked. The residents seemed to understand that opportunism was their only vehicle for high society's survival. If they did not utilize the talents of those who came and went within six months' time (for the obvious purpose of establishing residency for whatever legal reason—speedy divorce, tax evasion or the avoidance of state income tax altogether) then they would be no more than a whistle-stop town of fifteen thousand on the way to San Francisco. As it was, the place was much more sophisticated because of the so-called "temporaries."

It didn't take long for me to establish myself, either. Once I had enrolled Ruth in the grade school—she was eight years old; David was four—I looked into the women's societies for myself.

I found a good variety in the Twentieth Century Club, a women's group of some two hundred members that met in an ambling Mediterranean style home that fronted on the Truckee River. All of the other women's organizations took turns hosting a weekly program there, so that a new member like me was exposed to all the community work opportunities available in town. The third meeting that I attended was hosted by the Nevada Public Health Association, devoted to instructing new mothers in the medical and nutritional care of their babies.

"Our volunteers visit new mothers at home," the chairwoman stated proudly to the rest of us, seated in rows of straight-backed chairs that filled the expansive living room. "We teach them the proper way to bathe their babies, how to diaper them, feed them and burp them. We teach them how to weigh their babies, and provide average growth charts for both girls and boys. If the mothers have trouble with nursing their young, we try our best to offer instruction, provide a list of medical doctors, or offer them—" and here, she paused for dramatic effect, "the latest in off-the-shelf grocery products: Infant formula to be drunk from a bottle through a pliant, rubber, eh, nipple."

The room erupted in nervous titters. Under ordinary social circumstances, such a word was not uttered in polite company. But because of the nature of the presentation, the club leadership had rationalized that it would be permissible—just this once—before a ladies-only audience.

Later, I learned that the chairwoman's husband was manager of the Reno Grocery Company, the wholesale distributor for Procter and Gamble, a midwestern manufacturer of infant nutrients, among other things. So everyone out here really was an opportunist. No harm in that I suppose, as long as I knew it.

The Club's social opportunities were rich and varied, though I could not partake of the weekly bridge games, held on Saturday afternoons, nor could Isaac and I attend the quarterly dinner dances, scheduled, as they were, on Friday nights. As far removed as we were from home, we still upheld our religious observance and would not violate *Shabbos*. We kept a kosher home, though it was a more difficult task out here, without all the kosher groceries that I was accustomed to seeing on the shelf, so I had to improvise a bit. Isaac turned his head the other way. What was not strictly kosher, he did not want to know. We continued our daily observances: Isaac laid *tefillin*. We chanted daily prayers.

Things were spread out here. Most of the streets were wide and paved to facilitate motor car traffic. The public transporation was lacking, unlike the intricate systems at home. Without a motor car, I was isolated. I quickly sought a remedy.

"Isaac," I said seven weeks after the children and I had arrived. "I think the time has come for us to buy a motor car."

"Bella, Darling, you don't even know how to drive." He hardly looked up from the score he was studying.

"How hard could it be? All the other women do it. I shall learn," I said.

"I don't even know what a motor car costs," Isaac answered. "I don't know that we could afford such a luxury, especially seeing as we're only here for a time."

Was he counting the weeks already?

"I am perfectly willing to take in sewing jobs in order to help finance the machine," I said. "And when it is time to go back home, I will happily sell the vehicle. Without it, I am stuck at home. I find the house charming, mind you, but town is a good long walk away, far too far for a four-year-old's legs, and I almost always have David with me. So, what do you say?"

"Could I drive it sometimes, too?" Isaac feigned sheepishness to remind me of my tendency to dominate once I had made up my mind to do something.

"If you are good," I answered with a smile, acknowledging the lesson learned.

*

It took several more weeks before Isaac agreed to shop for a car. Reluctantly, he acquiesced to a Sunday afternoon family outing to visit with the gentlemen at Steinheimer Brothers.

I had spent the intervening weeks studying up on motor cars, and, based on what I had learned from the women at the Twentieth Century Club, I had already determined that a Studebaker Six sedan, priced around seven hundred and fifty dollars, was the suitable and appropriate family transport. Steinheimer's sold more of them, and at better prices, than any other motor car dealer in the states of Nevada and California.

But I did not disclose my advance decision to Isaac.

"Oooooh!" I gushed over a roadster in Steinheimer's big picture window facing Fourth Street. David pressed his nose to the glass.

"I bet it goes real fast," he said.

"Shhhhh," his big sister socked his arm.

"Oh, Bella, stop," said Isaac. "That contraption's hardly safe for you and the children. Look at how low it sits to the ground! Look at the size of the tires—so small! We have to think practically if we are to consider the purchase of a motor car."

"Your husband is right," a salesman had slithered up beside us and listened in on our sidewalk conversation. "After all, Madam, you and those beautiful children of yours make for mighty precious cargo."

"Why, thank you, Sir," I put on my best imitation manners. "Thank you very kindly for your genuine concern for our safety. I wonder, then, what type of a motor car would be suitable for family use?"

"Won't you step inside," he guided us into the Steinheimer's building, which consumed the entire block bordered by Fourth Street and Sierra, and steered us to the two sedans occupying the center of the sales room floor.

"Well, now, that's more like it," Isaac used his head-of-the-household voice. "That's what I call a piece of machinery!" He slapped the side of a shiny black vehicle.

"I couldn't agree with you more, Sir. She's the top of the line. She'll do upwards of seventy miles an hour on the open road—outside of town, of course. And there's plenty of gumption in her engine. Climbing the Sierras to head into California would pose no problem for this baby."

"I see," said Isaac, his enthusiasm waning ever so slightly. "And the price?"

"The price, Sir? Now remember, she's top of the line. The finest motor car manufactured by The Studebaker Company. She'll last you, too. She's reliable, all right, and that's a fact. She's listed at…"

The children began to scramble about, bickering in a quiet hum that crescendoed as the salesman uttered the critical piece of information. I strained to hear him as I clamped a hand on each child's shoulder, indicating that they should be still. Alas, I missed it, but Isaac, predictably, came to my rescue.

"Eight ninety-five, eh?" Isaac repeated.

"Isaac, when would we ever drive to California?" I was watching Ruth dawdle out of the corner of my eye, while keeping a sturdy hand on David. "I would be just petrified of those mountains," I emoted for effect.

"I would much prefer to take the train. Much prefer it. Oh, dear, just the thought of driving those mountain roads makes me queasy."

And I was off again, to chase down Ruth, who had strayed from my immediate view.

"Well, now, Sir, I did think I heard you say that safety was a primary consideration," the salesman raised his voice so that I would hear, too. "And this baby is the safest model on the road. Why, at high speeds you'll be comfortable and the solid body will absorb any shock."

"Shock? Oh, my!" I squealed, pulling Ruth across the room, back to where we were standing, conversing. "High speeds? Oh, no, no, no. I do not think you understand what we want. Just a nice, friendly little car for me to putter around town, that is all. Perhaps you could teach me to drive, Sir? I am a quick learner. But this car," I paused. I looked it up and down. "Well, it is so...*big*. And, as you say, so, so...*powerful*. It is much more than we need. There must be something else you could show us."

Now he gestured toward the Six.

"What about this little model over here?" he asked.

I recognized my choice at once.

"Well," I said, tentatively, "It *looks* more manageable."

"Well, then," the salesman perked up.

Isaac followed along.

The children were on the run again, but at least I could see where they were playing.

"This here is our Studebaker Six, a six-cylinder machine perfect for driving around town. She handles well. She's safe as can be. In fact, she might be just the thing for you, Ma'am, if you're to be the primary driver."

"Isaac?" I had to defer, of course, but now, at least, we were talking about the right model. All I had to do was steer Isaac to reach the same conclusion that I had.

"That seems more suitable for our needs," Isaac agreed.

But beyond that, he said very little. He stood, hands in pockets, looking at the sales room floor. I am afraid he was uncomfortable here, outside the realm of his knowledge base. In truth, we both were out of our elements. I was only spared from discomfort myself by having done my research in advance.

"And the price?" I asked, surveying the smooth, shiny lines of the two-door contraption with an ample back seat.

"Well, she's listed at seven ninety-five," he said.

"Hmmmmmm, " I said. "Seven ninety-five."

I looked at Isaac, who remained silent.

I said nothing, either, which left the salesman to speak if the silence was to be broken.

"But that's list," he began his patter, his pitch. "And there's certainly room to negotiate."

"Well," I said. "That is a relief. Because my friend Mrs. Wheeler—do you know the Wheelers? I believe her husband does something or other down at the bank—well, Mrs. Wheeler told me that she bought her Studebaker Six for considerably less than that!"

I had met Mrs. Wheeler through my work with the Public Health Association. The group paired older members with new ones for the newcomers' first few visits with new mothers, and she and I were paired together. After our maternity visit, she invited me to tea, and I had, indeed, inquired about her motor car, which was ever so comfortable and offered a smooth ride. We talked about our families, our husbands. I told her that Isaac was a musician, and she told me, with a degree of pride, that her husband, Sam, was an officer of The Reno National Bank. I had asked her, too, about learning to drive, and that is how I knew to ask the salesman for driving instruction.

"Oh, you're a friend of the Wheelers?" the salesman seemed newly interested.

"I suppose that you could say that," I answered demurely. "Mrs. Wheeler and I had tea just the other day…"

"Well, I'm sure we can work something out, indeed," said the salesman. "Indeed."

But by this time the children were awfully restless, and Isaac suggested that we call it a day. We left without the Studebaker, though I had the feeling it would not be long before I found myself seated behind the steering wheel.

*

Spring was approaching, and with it, Isaac's birthday. Ruth, especially, wanted to do something special by way of celebration. She had in mind a gift—something memorable, something meaningful, something that would "last and last," she said.

We decided to take some time to think on it.

Meanwhile, I, too, wanted to do something special for Isaac. He had, after all, agreed to come all this way just for me, and for such a length of time. And now, it appeared, we were about to buy a car at my urging. I wanted and needed to show my appreciation and my gratitude.

One day, during one of my strolls downtown, I happened to glance in Kuppenheimer's window. We had been out here several months already, and in all that time Isaac had bought nothing new for himself. I knew that he enjoyed dressing well, and I thought that he might like a new vest, or a tie, perhaps something with a western motif to remind him of our sabbatical here. I stopped in the store, to take a look.

"Why, Mrs. Grossman, how nice to see you!"

It was my newfound acquaintance, Mrs. Wheeler.

"Mrs. Wheeler! How nice, too, to see you! Are you shopping for your husband?"

"Why, yes, indeed. Please, let me introduce you," she said.

And from behind a rack came Mr. S.H. Wheeler of the Reno National Bank.

"Samuel H. Wheeler," she stated with formality, "Meet Mrs. Isaac Grossman, of the New York Grossmans," she said, although the name meant nothing to the non-Jewish world.

"Please," I extended my hand, "Call me Bella."

"A pleasure," he said.

"And for me," I answered, following proper protocol.

"Grossman, Grossman, now let me see," he was scratching the side of his head when I noticed that his unfinished pants did not match his coat. Apparently, I had caught him in the midst of a fitting. "I had an inquiry just this week about a Grossman," he continued. "Something about a motor car purchase, if I am not mistaken," he said.

Oh, how embarrassed I was to think that he thought that we had used his name in our pursuit of a motor car!

"Are you in the market?" he inquired.

"Well, as a matter of fact," I flashed my sincerest smile at his wife. "I enjoyed so much my outing in Mrs. Wheeler's Studebaker that my husband and I went looking at motor cars week before last, with our children."

"Oh?" He was too polite to ask directly how we had come to use his name as we shopped.

"Yes, yes," I continued, pretending not to notice his subtle annoyance. "Well, when the salesman asked if I had ever had the pleasure of riding in a Studebaker, I answered in the affirmative at once. I have never so much enjoyed a motor car ride as the one with Mrs. Wheeler when we called on one of the Assocation's new mothers."

"I see," Mr. Wheeler seemed assauaged, thank goodness. "Well, how did you find the motor car?"

"I found it quite to my liking, as a matter of fact, though I do not know how to drive," I said.

"Oh, the salesman can teach you," Mrs. Wheeler interjected with enthusiasm. "He taught me to drive, and I have hardly stopped since I learned," she laughed.

"What a splendid idea!" I answered, pretending to forget that she had already told me to ask for instruction as part of the price.

"So you bought the motor car?" Mr. Wheeler was curious. I supposed he wondered if we had secured our financing for the purchase from a lending institution other than his.

"No, not yet," I told him. "You see, we had our children with us. They are still small: Ruth is eight, and David is just four. They were so wound up with the sales room full of motor cars, so full of energy—children will be children, you know—that we were forced to leave before we could negotiate the sale, but we do intend to return to Steinheimer's, and very soon at that," I said.

"I see," Mr. Wheeler said, smiling now. "Well, you must know, Mrs. Grossman, that if you and your husband require financing, that we at The Reno National Bank would be more than happy to assist you." He handed me his calling card.

"Why, thank you, ever so," I said, knowing full well that ours would be a cash sale.

*

May 22, 1924

Dear Parents,

What a time we are having!

Isaac is the absolute toast of the town! The production of Gilbert and Sullivan's "H.M.S. Pinafore" that he directed at Ruth's school was so successful! He trained the children to behave so professionally that I think they surprised even their own parents! Ruth made a wonderful Buttercup. Oh, it was a little bit awkward at first: In the days immediately following the posting of Isaac's casting decisions, I sensed a slight under-current of resentment on the part of the other parents at the school, that Isaac's own daughter would play the lead. (I, of course, was not surprised in the least by Isaac's choice. You know how he loves to dote on Ruth!) But by opening night, most of the bad feelings had passed. We made a deliberate effort to make every child feel like a star, creating individual-ized costumes and make-up for each one. And once the others saw Ruth perform, no one could deny that she was right for the part. Her pitch was perfect; her delivery crystal clear. You should have seen her in her bonnet! Adorable!

The production was well worth the effort, though it took a good deal of work on my part to finish every costume in time. The last two nights I stayed up sewing into the wee hours of the morning. What a shame that you could not see the show, and what a shame that they only performed it four times. But then, Isaac will organize another, and it, too, will be wonderful, I am sure.

I find more and more of interest the longer that we stay in Reno. ~~I have made a new friend in Mrs. S.H. Wheeler, who directs the infant health care program that I wrote to you about in my last letter. I met her husband, a banker, the other day while shopping for a birthday gift for Isaac. Such nice people! We shall have to invite them to dinner one night, perhaps in celebration of Isaac's birthday next month.~~

I thought better of the last part that I had written, and scratched it out. I would have to recopy the letter once I was finished, but that was a small inconvenience weighed against upsetting my parents. They had never left New York; they did not know any gentile people. They would not understand striking up a friendship with a non-Jew. They did not understand that there were so few of us Jews here, and of such diverse histories, that it took more in common than just being Jewish to establish a friendship. Anyway, we would not be here that long. Mrs. Wheeler would not be a life-lasting friend. I did not need to mention her, at least not in a social context.

I continued:

The children sorely miss their cousins, their aunts and uncles, and most especially, you. It is difficult to make a festive *Shabbos* without a sizeable group to share it, but we have found our place in the *Chebra B'ris Shalom* Society, the only local Jewish group, which holds services in a nearby church and makes the best of things, given its small size. The members all so appreciate Isaac! He has made the services ever grander, filling the hall with prayer set to music. And they certainly have made our family feel welcome.

~~I am trying to talk Isaac into buying a motor car.~~ We went to look at Studebakers the other day, and there is one that I particularly liked. It is called a Studebaker Six because the engine runs on six cylinders, whatever that means. I rode in such a motor car recently, on my way to call on a new mother through the infant health care society I wrote to you about. It is an eminently manageable vehicle, even suitable for a woman to drive. I am hopeful that we will be able to scrape together seven hundred and fifty dollars soon to purchase a Studebaker Six of our own, and that by the time that I return to you, that I will be an adept driver!

I reread the last paragraph and struck the first line. My parents, I knew, worried about Isaac's demonstrative affection toward me, and about his willingness to provide for me the material things that I desired. Why intimate that the motor car was something I had to coerce Isaac to consider? Better that they should think we found mutual pleasure in our mutual interest in a motor car.

Beep! Beep!

The honking horn of a motor car interrupted my correspondence. I put down my pen, walked to the front window and pulled back the drape to see what the ruckus was all about.

There was Isaac, grinning broadly, behind the wheel of a Studebaker Six!

"Gather up the children, Bella! We're going for a ride!" He motioned for me to come.

I opened the window to holler back at him.

"A ride? Why, Isaac! What the…"

"It's yours, Bella! It's yours! Your driving instruction begins tomorrow. Meanwhile, I've figured her out for myself—nothing to it—and I want to take my family out motoring! Hop to! Hop to!"

Well, what a surprise! And to think that I thought that he lacked enthusiasm for the motor car.

I went inside to call the children, gathered my own wrap and a scarf, and piled into the Studebaker, smiling.

Things were going quite to my liking.

*

I was hand embroidering red trim for a white taffeta dress I was making for myself when Ruth approached, again concerned about a gift for Isaac. When she saw what I was doing, it was as if a light came on inside her head.

"Oh, Mama!" she cried. "You've given me the best idea! Could we, could we please, please, make a new *tallis* for Poppy? Do we have enough time before his birthday? I want it to be a special one, a very special one, one that would remind him forever and ever of our time in the West. Could we, Mama? Could we?"

I had to admit it was a wonderful thought.

Ever since Isaac had given his *tallis* away to the older gentleman at *shul*, he had wrapped himself for prayer in a coarse, cotton cloth, bought off a bolt in the general store. He had carefully tied the requisite fringes on the four corners of the rectangular fabric, but it lacked the decorative touches that Isaac prided himself in wearing in every other element of his clothing, and it lacked the special ring of distinction of the *tallisim* that my family made.

"What a wonderful, wonderful idea, Ruth!" I exclaimed, with animation and genuine enthusiasm filling my tone. "I think Poppy would love nothing more for his birthday. I am sure we could manage to make it by then!"

"Really? Oh, Mama! You are just the bestest ever!" Ruth hugged me tightly around the shoulders, her loose hair brushing against my cheek.

I glowed inside, with pride for my daughter's thoughtfulness, with joy and anticipation of sharing the project, and with love for my family.

*

Although Isaac spent all day at *shul* on *Shabbos*, I spent only the morning there. At noon I brought the children home to give them their lunch and to let them play freely during the long, lazy afternoons. I spent my time reading or resting, never working, for that would violate the law of the Lord.

In New York there were so many of us at home with children on *Shabbos* afternoons that we would eat our pre-prepared lunches together and spend our afternoons visiting, boasting of our children's accomplishments, trading neighborhood news, sometimes even discussing a book mutually read, while the children played with their friends, indoors through the long, cold winters, and outside, on the sidewalks in front of our Brooklyn Heights stoops, in the warmth of spring and summer.

I was reading quietly in my armchair, when Ruth approached me sheepishly.

"Mama," she lamented, "I have nothing to do."

"Why not play 'tea party' or 'store' with David?" My eyes did not leave the page of my book.

"Oh, Mama," she moaned. "He doesn't play right. He doesn't follow any of the rules. And at 'tea' he does not make a very nice guest. He spills almost every time!"

"Why not find a nice book to read, then?" I patted the wide seat cushion of my chair. "You can sit here, with me."

"But David will interfere," she objected. "He always wants to get into my things."

"I know, I know, Dear. But that is only because he looks up to you. There must be something you would like to do this afternoon, hmmmm?"

"Well," Ruth sidled up close to me. "There is something that I would like to do, Mama, but I don't know whether you will let me or not."

"What is it?"

"Go to the movie show?" she asked shyly.

"Ruth, you know that today is *Shabbos*, Honey. You know we do not go to shows on this day. This day was intended as a day of rest, and it is our duty to respect and praise the Lord, our God—every day, of course, but most especially this day."

"But, Mama," her eyes were begging me. "It's Mary Pickford. She's my favorite."

"Well, Ruth, there will be other shows. Besides, I am not sure you have enough money saved to buy a ticket to the movies. Hmmmm?"

"It's free!" Ruth exclaimed. "A rich man who lives in the town bought all the tickets to the show, and he's opening the doors and letting all the kids in for free today, just today, so you see, there won't be other chances to go with all my friends from school, and I wouldn't be breaking any rules about not spending money on *Shabbos*. Oh, please, Mama, please!"

"I don't know, Ruth. How would you get downtown, for goodness sake? I cannot drive the motor car today. Poppy would be furious with me!"

"Selma's mother, next door, she said she would drive. Oh, can't I go with her? Please? Please?"

I looked at the longing in my daughter's face, and I felt a pang of guilt for uprooting her, dragging her across the country, away from home, away from friends and relatives, away from a place where our religious practice was the same as that of everyone else. At home, she would have had plenty to do—playing with cousins and helping to prepare the festive evening meal for the extended family of aunts and uncles, and grandparents and cousins. Here, we were different. Here, she had few options. Here, she faced friends' questions, and even condemnation, when she was unable to participate in a Saturday outing. I sensed that our religion—beloved, sacred and so resonant with meaning to us—seemed to her to be a cinch instead of a sail. I did not want that. I wanted her to be proud of the ways of our people, and to find happiness, security, identity, and belonging in our ritual.

I looked at my watch. It was half past twelve. If the movie ran from one until three, Ruth could still be home before Isaac arrived home from *shul*. "Don't tell Poppy," I looked at her sternly and patted her on the rump. "Now run along, and hurry back before Poppy gets home, o.k?"

*

I put on my white ratine dress with red trim, my red taffeta hat and my red pumps to go into town. I had made the dress and hat; the white silk stockings and pumps were store-bought. I thought that I would do a little shopping before I met Isaac for a nice dinner out at The Grand Cafe. He already was in town, at the Congregational Church, training the children's choir for the High Holy Days coming up in the fall.

I felt as though everyone on the street was watching me as I made my way out of the Studebaker to the sidewalk, and I was at first, unsure whether I had made a mess of parking the car, or whether they were admiring my outfit.

I went to the silks section of the general store's fabric department, and began to select—by feel, not by sight—the material that Ruth and I would use to start Isaac's birthday present. It had to be white, or off-white, to be traditional, although there were no Jewish laws specifying the color. And Ruth had decided on blue embroidery, in the pattern of the Sierra skyline. No one at home would recognize it as anything but a zig-zag design, but for Ruth, and for Isaac, the jags and crags would forever remind them of our time in Reno. It was her idea, her lovely idea.

"Help you?" A clerk interrupted my thoughts.

"Oh, just looking at silks," I answered without looking up.

"For yourself?" he asked.

"Well, actually, no." I said.

"For your girl?"

"Uh, well, in a way. A little girl is going to sew it," I answered, smoothing my hands over the various bolts of cloth, paying him little attention.

"Whatcha makin', Darlin'?" he persisted.

"A *tallis*, for my husband, for his birthday," I said by rote, examining fabrics more closely now.

"A *what*?" His voice rose in pitch.

"A *tallis*." I repeated. I turned and looked at this funny little man, a hill-billy-sort whose efforts to strike it rich in the gold mines must have failed, and now, too old to chase further west, had resigned himself to living well enough on wages earned as a local shopkeep. "It's a prayer shawl," I explained. "A shawl that Jewish men wear when they pray."

"A shawl for prayin'? For a man?" He asked, incredulously. "A man is supposed to wear a silk shawl? Well, golly me, I thought I'd heard every-thing. Whatever will they think of next?"

And he walked away, slapping his thigh, bobbing his head.

We were so far from home.

*

"You look just marvelous," Isaac said to me when I entered the Grand Cafe. "We ought to have your picture taken, just so," and he framed up his hands like a photographer looking through a camera lens, imagining how the finished photograph would print.

It just goes to show that those fashion writers do not necessarily know what's what. They said that red shoes were out of style this year. Well, I say that red shoes look well any time if you have a suitable red outfit to go with them. And most of the restaurant patrons seemed to agree. Why, the looks I got as we followed the maitre'd to our table! I know that it is immodest to say so, but it was a wonderful feeling, indeed.

We dined on fish and baked potatoes. We were meat and potatoes peo-ple, but we did not eat meat in a restaurant. Unkosher. I found the fish savory, flaky and tender. Delicious. Somehow, when I made this same meal at home, it never tasted quite as good as it did in a restaurant. When I said as much to Isaac, he heartily disagreed with me.

"You're a wonderful cook, Bella. And a wonderful mother, I might add. Say, do you suppose you could ask the neighbor woman to watch the children again next week. I would love to take you to a show."

He was relaxed, he was happy, he was becoming all that I hoped that this sojourn would make him—a complimentary, attentive, and loving husband.

After cofee and a piece of chocolate cake, we strolled around the block, arm in arm, to the car.

"Isn't this nice?" Isaac asked me. "Let's loop around the block again before we head for home, eh?"

It seemed so natural to be here, so serene. The streets in this part of town were quiet, though I noticed that Isaac looked a long time up one alley, in which a couple of men stood huddled by a door.

We took the riverside route back to Ralston Avenue, and pulled off to the side of the road halfway home.

"I love a night like this," said Isaac, ever the romantic. "The moon shining over the water, wavelets licking at the river banks, a warm, fragrant breeze in the air, and you."

He leaned toward me and kissed me, then sat back to assess my reaction.

"May I?" he asked.

I could not deny him.

In his urgency, he knocked off my hat, rumpled my hair and wrinkled my dress, smacking wet kisses down my neckline. I felt a mess, but how could I say no? I adored the pretty words and all. But I had not realized how hungry he was.

"Isaac, Isaac," I collected myself. "It is getting late. We really must get home to the children, o.k.?"

"Well, if you insist," Isaac settled back over to the driver's seat and started the ignition.

*

When we walked in the door, our neighbor was rocking in the rocking chair, listening to the radio.

"Children are all tucked in, Mrs. Grossman. My, but don't you look pretty!" she said. "Ruth ate a nice big piece o' meat for dinner with a roll, but that David, he's a picky one, in't he? Well, he just wanted to eat his dessert. We had quite a little struggle there, but I managed to get a few bites o' good food down him before he got into that cookie jar.

"Postal delivery came while you were out, it's there on the table, alongside the newspaper. Well, good night, y'all. We'll see you when the sun shines bright."

What a lovely woman, so good-natured, and so good with the children. It was a stroke of luck to have found a house across the street from hers. I tried to compensate her extra, to take over samples of goodies I baked up, or leftovers too few for a family meal, but just about right for a single person.

Isaac headed toward the children's rooms to give them their good night kisses, while I flipped through the day's post: A magazine, a circular from Chism's Ice Creamery, a notice for a school board meeting, a letter to Isaac, postmarked "New York" in a hand that I did not recognize.

I was too tired to start opening mail. I took the newspaper with me to our room, took off my taffeta dress ensemble and slipped into my nightgown and into my bed. Isaac came along shortly.

"They o.k.?" I asked after the children.

"Sleeping like angels," he looked content.

He hung his suit on his wooden valet, wiped his shoes with a chamois cloth, placed them in the closet, and clambered into bed beside me. He reached across me, to turn off my bed light.

"Now, where were we?" he whispered, pulling my face close to his.

He pressed his hands down on my shoulders, kissing me, rubbing his torso against me, then straddling my waist, he sat upright.

"You don't mind, do you, Bella?"

I sighed. "Not in the slightest, my love. It's my pleasure," I answered as convincingly as I knew how.

He rocked back on his heels, slipped my long gown up to my shoulders and lay back down on top of me, skin to skin. He caressed my breasts, he massaged my middle, he placed his hand between my thighs. I was dry yet, but that did not dissuade him.

Soon, it was over, and Isaac was snoring beside me, looking as satisfied as a man who had just made love ought to look.

I went to the kitchen for a glass of water, and passed by the stack of mail again.

The letter addressed to Isaac was gone.

*

"So, you see, Honey, you pull the threads this way, and as you cut them away, the loose ones remaining make the fringe, you see? It is not very difficult, once you see how it is done. There, now we tie a knot, and there it is. One corner. All done. Isn't that pretty?" I waved the tasselled edge toward the light. "Now you try."

We were working together, Ruth and I, on the *tallis* that she would give to Isaac.

She worked diligently, carefully, her little brows knitted together in concentration. She did not want to make a mistake, though I had bought more than enough fabric to start again in the event that she did. And if she did not, well, I could always use it to make something for myself.

"Do you think Poppy will like it?" she asked as she worked.

"I know he will, Darling," I answered with approval.

"Do you think he will wear it?" she wondered.

"Of course, he will," I said.

I was so very proud of Ruth, and wanted her to know so.

"Do you think he will wear it, even in New York?" she eyed me somewhat suspiciously, as if to ask whether, not when, we would return home.

"I have no doubt," I reassured her. "This is a very special gift, more special than anything you could buy in a store, more special than most things that children can make.

"Now keep pulling. There, that's it. Now this one. No. Yes, that's the one. O.k. Good. And the knot…"

I missed home, myself, and wondered when it would be safe—or at least, safe enough—to go back.

*

They called him Omaha Bill, I suppose, because he hailed from Nebraska. He played Santa Claus year-round to the children of Reno, the sugar daddy who doled out candy on street corners, who laughed from the depths of his belly at their silly jokes, who bought out the Saturday matinee every now and again, and threw open the doors to kids of all ages.

A broad-bellied man in a stiff sombrero and leather coat, with a holster and a handlebar mustache, a bandana and black cowboy boots, he looked every bit the part of the wild westerner. Nobody knew where his money came from—whether from gold mines or railroads or livestock or land—but everybody knew he had plenty of it. He spent freely, even lavishly, and especially on the young ones. He was kind and gentle to them. But toward adults he was aloof, even reclusive. No one in town knew where he lived, and no one knew much about what he did. No one even knew his full name. He was just known as Omaha Bill. If he had not been so wealthy, and so generous, he might have been mistaken for a derelict, loitering, as he did, on the corner in front of the Riverside Bar, tossing back orange sodas, shooting the breeze with the locals.

When children sheepishly approached him, curious about this man of mythic proportions, whose goodness was broadcast by word of mouth, he crouched to their level to speak gently to them.

"If you can guess what I got in my pocket, it's yours!" his eyes would sparkle as he invited them to play.

"A handkerchief!" one child would say.

"A pocket watch!" another called out.

"A silver dollar!" cried a third.

And out would pop the silver dollar, into the eager hand of the child who had named it.

"We'll play again," Omaha Bill would say. "Come on back, some-time, y'hear?"

And the children would scurry off, giggling, with their loot.

*

Teaching Ruth to embroider was painstaking. Her little fingers were not quite limber enough to weave the needle in and out without leaving pin points in the fabric. She would stab the needle through the silk, then change her mind about its placement, and stab again, leaving a mark.

"Oh, no!" she cried. "I'll never get it!"

"Now, now. Have patience," I told her. "Try it this way." And I demon-strated my best technique. She tried again, but could not get it quite right.

"Oh, forget it, Mama!"

"Patience," I cautioned, evenly.

"I can't do it! I give up!" She threw the cloth at me, the needle dangling by a thick blue embroidery thread, and ran from the room in tears.

I gave her the time to cry out her frustration. I watched the clock on the wall for a full five minutes before I went to knock on her bedroom door. I remembered from my own youth feeling the fiery fit of tempera-ment building in my bowels, blazing in my groin, beating in my chest, overtaking, overpowering until I had no choice but to erupt in rage.

It was the longest five minutes I could remember. Each wail from Ruth begged me to come to her side, to hold her head in my lap, to rock her and hold her and tell her I loved her. But that would do nothing for her esteem, nothing to teach her first to accept, and then to control the uncontrollable heat that seared within all humankind. I hoped I could figure out how to comfort her, how to help her, how to assist her in com-pleting the embroidery herself. It would damage her pride if I finished stitching it for her. She needed to do this on her own.

"Ruth," I said. "Honey."

"Go away!"

"I think I have an idea," I said. "Will you let me come in and talk to you?"

"No!" She barked.

"Is that nice?" I asked.

"No," she softened. And then I heard weeping, muffled by pillows.

I turned the knob and went into the room. Ruth knelt beside her bed, her forehead resting on her forearm, her face buried in her bedspread. I patted her shoulder.

"It's all right, Honey. It's all right."

Her sobs soon became sniffles, and finally, she lifted her head from her arm and looked at me.

"I'll never get it!" she complained.

"Listen, I have an idea," I said. "Remember when you were a very little girl, how you tried to draw pictures of people, but could not manage to get them to look right?"

"Uh huh," she admitted.

"Well, remember what we did then? I drew the outlines in dark black crayon, and you colored the insides, all by yourself, making those people look just as you wished. Remember?"

"So?"

"So, what if I draw the mountains you want to stitch on Poppy's *tallis*? I could use a very light pencil, and you could follow the lines to make your stitches. Then afterward, if the pencil still shows, we can spot it out before we give it to Poppy. Shall we try?"

"O.k.," Ruth relented.

We returned to the living room, where she had thrown the *tallis*.

"Let me see," I said, picking up the fabric and spreading it over the kitchen table. I foraged through the adjacent drawer, looking for a pencil. Finding one, I returned to Ruth.

"Now, we are going to need a model for me to copy from," I said, glancing about the room at the books and magazines we had acquired in our months in Reno. I spotted the tourist book we had picked up from the Garden Hotel in anticipation of a motor car trip out to the lake. On the cover, there was a photograph of the Sierra Nevada in all its glory.

I began to outline the mountains, and soon had pencilled over the full length of the fabric.

"There," I said. "Now, try again."

And Ruth began again, arduously at first, but more nimbly as she went along. She concentrated on her stitches, cross stitches up the slopes, across the craggy peaks I had sketched and down the other sides of the hills.

"I think you are on your way, Darling. I am going to go into the kitchen to start dinner. But you call me if you need me, all right?"

"O.k., Mama," she said, deep in concentration over the work before her.

I began peeling potato skins into the sink, humming a little tune, and thinking to myself how very rewarding I found motherhood, after all. To be able to bring Ruth from tears to determination, and ultimately, I expected, to successful completion, was such a delight that I warmed inside. Then I heard her cry out.

"Ouch!"

Oh, dear, I thought. I ran to her side.

"I pricked my finger!" her sharp exclamation melted into a whimper.

"Let us rinse it in cool water to take out the sting. Come on now," and I scooped up my great big eight-year-old girl, who somehow still managed to fit like a babe in my arms when she was hurt or sick or vulnerable.

I set her up on the drain board, calmed her down and toweled her off, and she slipped off the counter to return to her work.

"Oh, no!" she cried when she picked up the cloth.

A small speck of blood, just the size of the needle point, dotted the Sierra design.

"I am sure it will wash clean, Honey," I said. "Do not worry. It will be all right. Poppy will love it, no matter what."

*

The drive to Pyramid Lake took just an hour. It was a quieter spot than the more famous Lake Tahoe—serene, pristine, the perfect place for contemplation.

But ours was to be a celebration, a family outing to wish Isaac well on the occasion of his thirty-third birthday. It was June 19, 1924.

I packed jelly sandwiches for the children, homemade chopped liver for me and Isaac, and birthday cake for everyone. We brought along our tennis racquets, hoping we might manage to rig up a court if we could find a smooth spread of grass. We brought a beach ball and swimming togs, and Ruth clutched a neatly-wrapped box to her chest.

David wanted in on the gift-giving as well, so we had made a mother-son trip to Kuppenheimer's, where David selected a red silk tie for his Poppy. It epitomized the showman in Isaac, and we both agreed that Isaac would enjoy it, especially on show nights, when all eyes were on him as director. David's box lay on the floor of the back seat of the car. The excitement of the picnic adventure had overcome his interest in presents.

Although I was a better driver than Isaac, he always took the wheel when we rode the motor car together. I could see the pitfalls coming way before Isaac recognized them, and I bit my tongue so as not to annoy him with my warnings, all the while thinking to myself, "Slow down!" "Brake!" "Look out!" "See the pothole in the road there? Steer clear!" I pushed the butt of my hand against the dashboard to support me through Isaac's bumps and jerks, and I prayed that the children would be all right, rolling about the back seat as they were, like a couple of billiard balls banking off of the upholstery, and off of each other.

Sharp twists and turns in the road made me queasy.

"Are you all right back there, children?" I asked Ruth and David over my shoulder.

"Yes, Mother," Ruth answered politely.

"Uh huh," said David. We had a ways to go on his manners.

I kept wishing the ride would be over, for I felt a wave of nausea wash over me.

"Isaac, could you take it a bit gentler on the curves?" I asked in my sweetest voice.

"Who's driving this motor car, Mother?" He answered, gaily whipping around yet another bend.

I clutched my stomach, but uttered not another word.

By the time we arrived at the lake, I was too ill to appreciate its splendor, much less to prepare our picnic spread. I excused myself from the rest of the group, and took myself on a short walk in the woods. Inhale. Exhale. Inhale. Exhale. Inhale. Exhale. Fresh mountain air filled my lungs until slowly, slowly, I shed my woozy wobble, regained my balance, and rejoined my family.

"Anyone hungry?" I called out with little oomph.

David was knee-deep in the lake. His shoes and socks lay neatly by the shore, as Isaac instructed him in casting out a fishing line. Ruth, still holding her gift box tight, had shaken out the picnic blanket, smoothing each corner on the grass, just so, in preparation for our party.

I laid out the napkins, the flatware and plates, and hailed the hearty group to the makeshift table I had prepared.

"Which would you like first, Isaac, presents or lunch?"

Isaac looked from Ruth to David and back to Ruth, who was bursting to forfeit her gift to her father.

"Ruth?" Isaac asked her. "You're my big girl. You decide."

"Presents!" she squealed, extending her box toward Isaac.

"No, mine!" said David, offering his.

"That's not fair," said Ruth.

"Now, now," Isaac calmed them. He was enjoying this interplay with the children. "How about drawing straws?"

He plucked two blades of grass from the lawn and hid their lengths inside his fist, letting just the pointy ends poke out.

"Whoever picks the long one wins," he said. "Ruthie, you pick first."

She yanked out a blade that, sadly, looked all too short to me.

"David?" And it seemed as though David pulled for an eternity, Isaac released the blade of grass so very slowly. But, at last, David held it up, and Isaac proclaimed him the winner. Ruth looked downcast.

"Now, Ruth, you can't complain," Isaac said. "After all, you had first pick. Now, no moping on my birthday, eh? There, that's my big girl." He elicited a smile.

Isaac quickly untied the bow on David's box and slipped off the top. He crinkled the tissue.

"Hmmmmmm," he said. "Now what have we here?"

And he pulled out the tie with a great, "Aha!"

"Why, David, what a wonderful gift! Thank you, my boy! It's just perfect, don't you think, Belle? Isn't it just me?" And he posed, holding it in front of his neck, letting it drape down to his belt, extending his other arm as if he were about to take a bow. Then he slipped off the tie he had worn that day, and knotted the new, red one round his neck.

"Well, isn't that fine?" he asked. "Just fine. Thank you, my boy. Thank you very much."

And then he turned to Ruth.

"Have you a gift for Poppy, too?" he asked.

"Uh huh." She had not quite gotten over losing at straws. "Happy birthday, Poppy." And she ceremoniously handed Isaac the box that she had wrapped herself. The paper was crooked, and the bow was lopsided, but Isaac beheld the box as if it were the most beautiful package he had ever seen.

"Well, well, well," he said. "This is quite something. Quite a tidy wrapping job, Ruth. Now, let's see what's inside."

He slipped the ribbon off the box and lifted the tape that held the paper in place. Then, ever so slowly, he lifted the lid. Jocularity fell from his face, and solemnity replaced it.

"Oh, my," he gasped, with discernible emotion. "Oh, Ruth. Oh, my."

He lifted the *tallis* from the tissue-lined box, and held it up to the sunlight. A tiny tear rolled down his cheek. He dabbed it away.

"It's bright today, eh?" he said by way of explanation. "Oh, Ruth, Ruth, it is beautiful. I shall treasure this *tallis* always. Always."

And he took the prayer shawl and wrapped it around Ruth, pulling her close to him in a private hug as he encircled himself with it too, and whispered so that I could barely hear:

"May the Lord bless you and keep you. May the Lord make his countenance to shine upon you and be good to you. May the Lord shine on you, and bring you peace."

It was the ancient, priestly blessing, invoked, parent to child, on the sabbath, and uttered by rabbis over gatherings of Jews as they parted ways. Our rabbi at home raised his hands over the congregation and spoke the priestly blessing at the end of each service, when we retreated to our separate lives until the next week, when we would, God willing, be reunited in prayer again.

When the two parted, Ruth was quick to point out and apologize for the tiny red spot on the shawl. I had been unable to wash it out without scarring the silk.

"It only makes it that more special," Isaac said. "Blood comes from the heart. And so does this gift." He looked hard into her eyes. "I love you, Ruth," he said quietly, before David broke the sanctity of the moment.

"Let's eat!"

*

Ruth approached me with skepticism.

"I know what you are going to say, Mama, but I have to ask you, just in case…" she began.

"What is it, Ruth?" I was up to my elbows in the butter that comes midway in churning milk to cheese, stroking it off of the churn so that I could begin the motion again. I had learned to home-churn cheese last month, at a Twentieth Century Club meeting on self-sufficiency. A woman from one of the Homemakers' Clubs had made a presentation explaining that, given sufficient land and manpower, we each could provide for our own daily needs, without need of grocery stores, dairies and the like, but by determination and self-reliance. What such a notion would do to the economy I could not imagine. But I thought I would try my hand at cheese, and send a brick back home to my parents.

"It's that Omaha Bill," Ruth could barely contain her glee. "He's done it again! Rented out the Majestic. The Majestic! Poppy's theater! On Saturday. I know, I know that it's *Shabbos*. But Mama, it's not like *Shabbos* at home. There's nothing to do here. There aren't any other Jewish children, except David. And all my friends from school are going. I could get a ride again, so that you wouldn't have to drive. Oh, Mama, please say 'yes,' please? I promise I won't tell Poppy, and I promise to be home before sundown. Please?"

"Ruth, grab that towel and wipe my forehead for me, will you?" My hands were slick with fresh butter and I was perspiring, the churning motion had been so strenuous. "Thank you. Much better. Yes. Thank you."

"Oh, Ruth. You know that that one time was an exception to the rule."

I glanced out the kitchen window, and saw Ruth's school friends huddled across the street, clustered near an oak, waiting, I knew, for my verdict. I was torn. My daughter wanted so badly to go, to be with her friends, to be like everyone else. And although she was different—she was Jewish, and they were not—she was not going to live her life here, where she would have to behave differently to prove piety. Soon enough we would return home, where everyone we knew was Jewish. Why should her time here be unhappy?

"Mama?"

"You will get a ride with Selma, or with one of your other friends?"

"I will, Mama."

"You will be home before Poppy comes home?"

"I promise."

"And you will not tell Poppy where you have been?"

"Never. I swear."

"All right, then. I do not suppose there is any harm in it, so long as no one—" and here, I rolled my eyes toward the front door to indicate clearly that I meant her father—"so long as no one finds out about this. Otherwise, Ruth, we are both in big trouble."

"Oh, thank you, Mama! Thank you!" Ruth grabbed my waist and swung me around, squeezing me in a tight embrace. I held my hands up, at ear level, to avoid getting butter all over her and myself.

When she ran out the side door to tell her friends that she could go, she suddenly looked so grown up to me. Her legs were long and lanky as they carried her away. Her hair flew in long tresses behind her as she ran. She gestured enthusiastically when she spoke.

Alas, I thought, cursing my buttery hands. I did not hug my girl good-bye, and now, the moment was lost; it was too late: She was not a baby any more.

*

With the summer gone and the High Holy Days upon us, Isaac entered a period of indefinable pathos. He brooded. He seemed unable to shake off the dark melancholy that hung over him like a rain cloud on the verge of a downpour, holding in every drop, swelling to bursting. Perhaps it was his conscience; perhaps it was the contrast between past and present.

At home, the High Holy Day preparations consumed him in zesty momentum. He had three or four choirs to train, and most years, aimed to compose a new piece of music for each of the full-house congregations that crowded the various *shuls* for both *Rosh ha Shanah*—the Jewish New Year, and *Yom Kippur*—the Day of Atonement.

This year, Isaac did not fret over his multiple choirs—there was but one for him to train. He did not have to juggle special rehearsals, nor did he agonize over new compositions. His reaction toward the season was bitter-sweet: He seemed relieved and pained at the same time. It is hard to describe his moodiness. I did my best to stay out of his way.

Much as we tried to sugar-coat it, our sabbatical was a mental and a physical exile from the mainstream of our way of life. It was as though we had been paddling along, in live, active waters for many years, and suddenly, we were diverted inland to a stagnant pond, where we rowed just as hard as we had before, but did not go as fast or get as far, and where there were no currents to carry us forward when we ran short of gusto of our own. From our little pond, we watched other vessels rushing by, but our own boat had slowed to inertia.

Our life was not what it had been.

We could not fish for the big fish way out there, where the white water swirls and the currents are swift. Here, we cast our lines in the still waters, close to shore, and tried to be grateful for what we could catch.

*

Slam!

"The nerve!" I could hear Isaac raging from where I stood, in the back bedroom, where I was sorting the clothes that the children had outgrown. Could it have been a year already? I remembered David wearing the winter clothes that I brought from New York, but now, the weather had turned cool again, and his thicker trousers were too tight through the waist, too short in the leg.

"Isaac?" I scurried to the hallway to gauge his demeanor.

"What a clod!"

Yes, rage. I was right.

"What has happened to upset you so?" I asked, leaving the chores for later and joining Isaac in the front room.

"They told me to work on *Shabbos!*" he bellowed. "The Sabbath! The Lord's day!" He was seething.

"Surely, you told them that you could not?" I fished for the rest of the tale.

"Surely, I did," Isaac mocked me. "Surely, I told them that I did not work on Saturdays, and what was wrong with the regular Saturday organist?"

"And?" I asked.

"And," Isaac continued, "He has been given a paid vacation, to San Francisco, in appreciation of his five years of service. The manager intended to close the theater on the days that he was scheduled to work, but this ragamuffin, this scalawag, this Omaha Bill, as he is called, has thrown a monkey in the works!"

"How, Isaac?"

"How? This Omaha Bill character, whoever he is, routinely buys out the theater and invites all the town children to the show for free. This, at the Saturday matinee, I am told. So, now he's done it again, and told all the children, only this Saturday, the Saturday for which he bought out the house, the organist is on vacation. That's why they told me to come to work."

"Well, they will just have to find somebody else."

"For a lot more shows than just this Saturday's, I'm afraid. When I refused to come in this Saturday, they told me not to come in at all."

"Oh, Isaac," I said. "I am so sorry."

I stood to console him, to wrap an arm around his shoulder, to let him bury his face on my breast. We were in the midst of an embrace, when we heard Ruth arrive home from school, distraught.

"Mama!" she hollered from the front of the house.

Isaac, ordinarily, would have been at work.

"Mama, they've canceled the free movie show!" She was on the verge of tears, when she noticed her father standing there.

"Poppy!" she said with some alarm.

"And what do you know of the free movie show?" he challenged her.

"Oh, um, uh, nothing," she said, looking to me to help.

"You seem as though you are disappointed," Isaac pressed her. "As if it would matter to you, whether there was a free movie show on *Shabbos*, or not."

He looked at me, accusingly. He looked at Ruth with anger.

"Which one of you is going to tell me how it is that my daughter concerns herself with a free movie show on *Shabbos*? Bella? Ruth?"

"I am sorry, Isaac," I began. "It really is all my fault. When I heard the women at the Club talking about this Omaha Bill character, and all the good that he does for the children of Reno, and when I noticed that the women talking about the movie show were the mothers of Ruth's friends, well, I did not see how it could hurt to let her participate in a little fun while we are away from our home, away from our customary habits, as part of our western adventure."

"Nonsense!" Isaac hollered. "It makes no difference where we are, we do not forget who we are! We do not break the law of the Lord! If we have slipped so far that even you, Bella, have forgotten that the very core of our existence lies in our adherence to our tradition, then I have only one thing to say."

Ruth and I leaned close and listened as Isaac pronounced our sentence: "Pack the bags, Bella! We are going home!"

AMALIA

"They're coming home!" Joshua told me.

I had no doubt who he meant.

I was grateful that Ike had arranged for me and Joshua to be together, at first for no other reason than to fill my time. Without Joshua for company, the year would have been unbearable. As it turned out, Joshua was no threat to Ike's relationship with me. I couldn't say whether Ike knew that for sure or not. But once the truth was told between me and Joshua, once we each knew the other's sexual secret, we had a fine time together, with no expectations, and no resultant disappointment, frustration or awkwardness. In time we grew close—as close as two friends can be, as close as I've been to anyone, but Ike.

Joshua understood the logistics of a secret life better than anyone I'd ever known, perhaps because he had learned by necessity how to maintain a secret life of his own. He was compassionate; he willingly shared with me the letters that Ike sent to him, describing the town, the work, the people, the scenery, his activities and his children. Ike was a prolific and colorful writer. I was sad that he could not write me directly. But my nieces might have found the letters, which would have confirmed their long-held suspicions, would have provided tangible evidence of the *shanda* I brought on the family. No, that would not do at all, especially given the pretense of my courtship with Joshua. Nor could I correspond directly with Ike, for the very obvious reason of Bella. And presuming that Ike might share Joshua's letters with Bella, or worse, that Bella might open the post in Ike's absence, Joshua could make no mention of me. So it was a one-way channel of communication, and if I had been offered the choice of sender or receiver, I would have picked the seat I was handed. Not knowing might have done me in.

As it was, it was all I could do to keep silent myself. I only wrote to Ike once in that year, and even as I wrote the note, sealed the envelope, licked the stamp, each and every step of the way, I knew I shouldn't have been doing it.

I couldn't help myself. I missed him so much. I knew I risked discovery, but, on the other hand, there was a part of me that wanted Bella to know I was still in the picture, that wanted to yank the covers off of their neat and tidy facade of family bliss. I wished the children no harm, I most truly did not. But her. Well, I resented her acting like all was well between them, and I resented his encouraging her to believe that it was. So I wrote an innocent enough little note, an update on my comings and goings. No hint of romance, only an "I miss you. Love, Amalia" at the end. I never did hear back.

"Back? When?" I could hardly contain my enthusiasm, though with Joshua I didn't have to.

"His letter doesn't say, exactly," said Joshua, scanning the page with his index finger.

My heart started racing. I knew not what to expect. What had precipitated the decision to return? Would we reunite, or would I not hear from Ike? Would he surprise me, or would he avoid me?

"But between the two of us, I suppose we'll find out soon enough," Joshua said.

BELLA

Long Island was a long way out.

It was lovely, suburban, with sprawling lawns full of neighborhood children, with spacious houses begging for fresh furnishings, with a large and lively Jewish community that welcomed us back to a life that we knew, a life that we loved, a life that we had missed desperately.

Still, I had been ambivalent about the return: Happy, of course, to come back home to family, to friends, to the familiar ways of a lifestyle ingrained through generations of living it, but reluctant, too, to raise the specter of Amalia, to invite the possibility that she would once again inhabit our home, even if invisibly. Toward the end of our stay in Reno I had almost forgotten her. Many a day she did not enter my thoughts. Moving back brought her to the forefront anew, raising fears, and doubts, and my own insecurities.

Much of my fear was allayed when Isaac agreed without hesitation—in fact, with some enthusiasm—to rent the two-story house in Arverne. We saw it on a blustery day typical of New York in January. Tumble-down snowmen stood on white lawns, some melted from yesterday afternoon's sun, and others abandoned by busy little mittens that, soaked through with snow and too cold to work on, were peeled off to bare small hands red with cold, eager for steaming mugs of cocoa. Slimy slush lay in the roadsides and the air smelled rich, like burning oak, so many chimneys were spewing smoke from fireplaces ablaze below.

It looked like a place where families thrived.

Thirty days later we moved in, enrolled the children in the Hebrew day school, rekindled friendships with the few families that we knew from Brooklyn, who had moved out to the island in the year that we were gone. I spent my initial weeks converting yet another house into a home, shopping, sometimes with Mother, sometimes alone, for furnishings, wallpapers, draperies—traditional trappings that looked like other families' heirlooms—in my heartfelt attempt to create a comfortable place that would feel like ours.

We had sold the Studebaker before we left Reno, and did not intend to drive a motor car in New York. We knew our way around town by public transit well enough, and Isaac and I agreed that a motor car would only cost us the additional expenses of gasoline, maintenance, and a parking garage. I expected that we would make our life on Long Island, that Isaac would string his jobs together here instead of in the city, and that the distance from Manhattan would inhibit him from rekindling his previous romance.

But, as was so often the case with me and Isaac, my prediction of how things would turn out turned out to be exactly wrong.

He did not seek work on Long Island at all.

No, he went back to Brooklyn, to the Hebrew Educational Society, where the director gladly took him back.

He went back to Kane Street, where his brother, the rabbi, embraced him with enthusiasm at Congregation *Bais Yisroel Ansheimes*.

He went back to the Lower East Side, to the Hebrew Educational Alliance, where he was welcomed back with happy handshakes.

Travel time to these jobs was not insignificant. The children and I saw less and less of Isaac, as he left the house earlier and earlier, and came home long after we all had gone to bed. The children's homework became my domain, along with the cooking, the cleaning, the laundry, the finances, and all of the other domestic chores. It was not long—perhaps a month or two—before I received the first of many evening telephone calls.

"Bella?" asked the voice on the phone.

It was Isaac.

"Bella, it's so late, Darling, and I have an early appointment tomorrow. I'm going to stay in town tonight."

"But..."

"Didn't want you to worry, Darling."

Click.

The phone went dead in my trembling hand.

We were back, all right, and so was my recurring nightmare.

AMALIA

I could hardly believe Ike was staying the night.

We had to take a room, of course. He couldn't stay at my nieces' place, especially since they still believed that Joshua and I were a romantic pairing. (Sometimes I wondered how thick-headed they could be? It seemed so obvious to me that we would not, and could not, be lovers.) I used Joshua as my excuse, telling my family I was going upstate overnight, to accompany him on a business conference, staying in separate rooms, of course.

Ike had a way of re-entering my life—rewiring the heart he had disconnected, relighting the soul he had disimpassioned, rehydrating the carnal well run dry. It was brilliant the way he had worked things out, resettling his family in the suburbs, resuming his professional life in the city, rekindling our love affair, no doubt, for all time this time.

We had enjoyed more than our fair share of "first times," but this time, for the first time, I felt real commitment. He didn't say anything to lead me to such a conclusion. I think it was more the way he looked at me, the way he held me, as if for dear life, as if he would never, never let me go.

"I could not bear being away from you," Ike told me over a candle light dinner.

The restaurant was Italian, a charming little place with red checkered tablecloths, frayed at the edges, with candle wax dripped over wine bottle centerpieces corked with red and green colored candles, with recorded accordion music blaring too loudly over tin speakers overhead. The place reeked of garlic and olive oil.

We slurped our spaghetti bathed in red sauce. Neither one of us knew how to twirl the long, skinny noodles around the fork the way the Italians do. It didn't matter, anyway. There was no one around to frown on our manners, no one to watch us watching each other, offering each other droopy forkfuls of food like the couples in love in the movie shows. Only our paper bibs spoiled the scene, but without them we would have been drenched in pesto and tomato sauce well before our plates were clean. And after a few glasses of wine, who noticed? We hazily, lazily, rewrote the scene as we played it, omitting its imperfections as we quaffed the kosher red wine we brought with us. The family who ran the place took no offense. Their place was, after all, situated on the border between the Jewish and Italian neighborhoods. They accepted our dietary laws, even if they did not understand them. They were happy enough to pour meatless spaghetti sauce over our noodles, and to pour the kosher wine we brought, charging just a small corkage fee to cover the cost of washing the glasses.

Our slow dinner over, we strolled up the street, to a small boarding house that rented rooms by the night. It, too, was run by an Italian family—cozy, hospitable, clean and accommodating. And we would not bump into anyone we knew there. I stopped in the bath on the way to our room. Ike went ahead down the hall without me.

I was nervous. But why?

Ike had made no mention at dinner of the year in Reno, whether he had successfully established residency, whether he had looked into divorcement from Bella. I had to know: Were we any closer to being together than we had been when he left? Or were we still adrift, in love but in limbo because of a decades-old promise that should not have been kept?

I padded down the well-worn carpet and tapped on the door of the room we had rented.

Ike pulled me inside, closed the door tight behind me, locked fiery lips on top of mine while feisty hands fidgeted to free me of my frock. He leaped on me like a hungry leopard. His tongue darted inside my mouth, making a loopy, circular motion, arching to engage mine in an oral fencing match. He tore at my clothes like a cat clawing a scratching post. He pushed me onto the bed, lowered himself on top and kneaded my bare breasts like bread dough. Ravenously, he pushed up my skirt, pulled my panties aside, massaged me until I grew moist down there, until my hips began rocking, eager to welcome him in.

If our dinner was slow motion, our lovemaking was a high-speed race.

Ike stripped off his suit and ducked under my dress, kissing my lower lips until they flared with desire for him. He did not fully undress me, just pulled my blouse open and pulled my skirt up, pulled off my panties and pressed on top of me, penetrating, pumping, until we were spent.

Exhausted, he rolled off me, pulled my head down to rest on his chest, stroked my face, my hair, my perspiring flesh.

"I'm sorry," Ike panted. "I just couldn't wait. Next time, I promise, I'll be more gentle."

"It's all right," I answered, running my hand the length of his torso. "I love it that you love me fiercely."

BELLA

If Arverne were not far enough from the city, the Catskills certainly would be.

I read about The Flagler resort in *The Forvitz,* the Yiddish-language newspaper that had been the principle source of information around our house ever since I was a girl. When I married and moved into my own home, I naturally subscribed, and Isaac often had a second copy with him when he came home at the end of the day. He could not wait until night-time to read the news. It was the best paper for news and perspectives of the Jewish community. My favorite section was the *Bindl Briefs,* where readers, mostly new immigrants, wrote in about their lives, their losses, their hopes and dreams. My parents, the first generation to come to America, made sure to teach me to speak and read Yiddish, in part so that I could partake of the *Forvitz.* God bless them. By the time I had grown to adulthood, many of those in my generation had lost the language, a loss that left them handicapped in many discussions of the Jewish issues of the day. I will always be grateful to my parents for insisting that I learn the language of the old country.

The advertisements for the Flagler, in Fallsburgh, about a hundred miles from the city, boasted of grounds spacious enough to accommodate lawn tennis courts and croquet courses, and even a nine-hole course for golf. A former farmhouse purchased by two Jewish businessmen and converted into a resort, the hotel had eighty guestrooms, with fifty baths, hot and cold running water and a telephone in every room. It had a lobby, a sun parlor, even an elevator.

Pictures in the *Forvitz* showed a grand, stucco exterior topped by parapets and gables of a baroque style. French windows modeled after Louis XIV's palace at Versailles invited sunlight to stream into the first-floor sitting rooms.

It was dazzling. But what really caught my attention was the description of the hospitality awaiting the paying guests: "Organized shows each night of the week, and impromptu entertainment by day." Might the hotel management offer a full-time wage to someone who could fill both bills, I wondered?

My letter of inquiry was met with a hopeful response: According to a job description the resort owners sent to me, the social director ran all of the guest activities, day in and night out. His qualifications included the ability to sing, to dance, to tell stories, to arrange parlor games, to plan hikes, to organize community sing-alongs at the campfire, to *kibbitz* with the guests, to mesmerize the children, to entertain in the dining room during meals, and to organize full-scale stage shows for each evening. His job was no less than to keep the guests from getting bored with their card playing, sun bathing or nature viewing.

I thought Isaac would be perfect for it.

My ulterior motive was simple: To separate Isaac and Amalia.

"Isaac," I began our evening conversation. I was sewing. He was reading.

"Isaac, I just read about the most wonderful place. It sounds like *the* place to spend the summer, and with Hebrew school out of session and your stage groups on hiatus, I wondered whether we might look into it."

"What?" said Isaac. As was typical these days, he had not been paying attention to me, and so I had to repeat myself.

"Bella, these resorts are for the wealthy, not for people of our means," he dismissed me.

"Isaac, I was not thinking of going as guests. I was thinking of your many talents, and the fact that summer is a slow time for you professionally. I hear that the resort owners hire social directors to run the guest activities in the summer, to stage shows every night and to socialize with the guests, to dance with the women and tell jokes with the men, and sing and tell stories with the children. I can think of no one more skilled than you to do any one of those things, let alone anyone capable of doing all of them."

"Heh?"

"Here, look." I pulled out the letter from Flagler's to show him the job description that the owners, Asias Fleisher and Phillip Morganstern, sent me.

"Interesting," Isaac uttered, reading the page. "But I don't know…"

"Maybe there might even be time to compose. It is so beautiful in the mountains. So inspiring."

"Bella, please…"

"Say you will inquire about it," I implored him. "What harm could there be in an inquiry?"

"We'll see, Darling. We will see."

*

Two days later I found the advertisement from the *Forvitz* clipped and laid neatly atop Isaac's dresser.

He had circled the words, "Glatt Kosher," tucked in the corner, in small type.

*

"Bella!" he bellowed. The front door slammed shut. "Bella? Darling? You're brilliant! Darling? Where are you? Bella?"

I wiped my hands on my apron skirt, full of flour from kneading our *challah*, and scurried in from the kitchen to answer Isaac's call.

"Bella! It's fabulous! You were right about Flagler's! Oh, what a summer it's going to be!"

"Tell me!" I enthused. I could hardly wait to hear.

"Well, last week I phoned up those men, Fleisher and Morganstern. It happens they were planning to be down in the city today on business. I met them. And you'll never guess."

He did not allow me the time to guess.

"You're looking at Flagler's new social director!"

"No!"

"Yes! And such a deal! Two hundred dollars for the season. That's what they call it in the mountains, 'the season.' Plus room and board. And that's not all."

"What? More? Tell me!"

"For two weeks at the end of the summer, you and the children can come up to join me as guests, all expenses paid for you, too!"

My heart swelled until I nearly cried. In fact, I felt my cheeks grow hot—from surprise, from joy, from an unexpected and newfound sense of Isaac's appreciation for my worth as a wife. That Isaac had asked that provisions be included for me to join him at the resort was so much more than I would have hoped for, even more than I would have thought to ask for myself. It filled the lonely cavity that ached so often within my chest that I had grown accustomed to the empty place where love should be.

I had merely wanted him away from Amalia.

He had wanted to be with me.

AMALIA

That first Flagler's summer was tough on us.

It took Ike weeks to get into the swing of summer at Flagler's. The guests' round-the-clock amusement required Ike's round-the-clock attention. While they were resting, recovering from the day's activities, Ike was still working, dreaming up new ways to entertain them for the week while finalizing the next day's plans. And oh, the surprises awaiting him there! He wrote me (care of Joshua), for example, that untold to him until he reported to Flagler's for work, the social director was required to do double duty, as a waiter or bus boy when the kitchen came up short on staff. He was furious!

"They treat me like a schoolboy," he wrote about the resort's more pompous guests. "'Sonny, get me a little more sugar, heh?' and tipping me a nickel for my trouble, as if I were a kid, with no education, no profession, no livelihood, as if I depended on their gratuity to take my girl out to the weekend picture show.

"Some, of course, are nicer than others," his letter continued.

> There is one family I have grown quite fond of. The Kaufmans. Perhaps you know them. They live in Brooklyn, but do not worship at Kane Street. The children are sweet, and so bright and talented. They take direction very well. I plan to cast them in the leads of the mid-summer musical, which will be *Hansel and Gretl*. Mrs. Kaufman is quite a lady, and so very patient, not unlike you, Mal, though nowhere near as beautiful. She stays here with the children during the week, and her husband joins them on the weekends. He is a doctor, and although he could afford it, his kind heart does not permit him to leave ill

patients for pleasure's sake. I believe the Kaufmans will spend the whole summer here. I hope that they do. I like all of them.

I miss you like crazy, Mal, and hope that we can arrange some time together before summer's end, when I will focus my energy on High Holy Day preparations. I am grateful the holidays are late this year. I will need the time to train the choirs, though I doubt that I will find time to write any new music for them this year.

Ever your adoring,

Ike

Kaufman. Kaufman. I searched my memory, but came up blank. The name sounded vaguely familiar to me. Well, even if I didn't know them myself, surely, I must know someone who did.

I put down Ike's letter and went to make tea. I was suffering from my monthly cramps. I had such an uncomfortable time of it.

I sat at the kitchen table waiting for the water on the stove to boil.

Dr. Kaufman. Dr. Kaufman.

And then I remembered.

Kaufman was the name of the doctor I saw just before I lost our child.

BELLA

Isaac cast us all in his final production, a spoof that was legendary in the Catskills: The Mock Wedding. I was the groom and Isaac played the bride. The skit's humor lay in the reversal of roles, but few female guests wanted the masculine part. I did not want to play a man, either, but I was willing to comply. After all, I was a guest of the management. It seemed a small price, to do my part. David was the bridesmaid and Ruth the groomsman. Guests played the guests, the musicians, the mother and father of bride and groom. Mr. Morganstern played the rabbi. He looked the part, in his black robe and black beard. By the time Isaac came down the aisle in his white gown and tulle veil, the entire resort was astitch in laughter.

They cheered him.

They loved him.

It was fun to be the one who was with him.

Isaac had grown so close to the summer guests that he could create inside jokes tailored to their professions, their situations and their individual senses of humor. The management strictly forbid political jokes, or jokes touching on any area of potential controversy. Isaac was told to stay within the bounds of inoffensive, topical humor, which usually dealt with weather, or travel, or, at the very edge, the *goyim*. All of the guests at the resort were Jewish, so none took offense at jokes about gentiles.

"With all the strife between Jews and gentiles, you have to wonder, why did God create *goyim*, anyway?" Isaac, as emcee, would ad lib into the microphone.

The audience smiled in anticipation. They knew a punchline was on the way.

"Well, somebody's got to pay retail!" he said to roars of laughter, particularly among the guests in the *schmatte* business—the garment industry, or rag trade, as it had come to be called on the Lower East Side.

So skilled was Isaac at endearing himself to the people around him, that when he came on stage at night, whether as bride, or emcee, or musician or clown, the guests cheered him like parents applauding their own precious child.

Toward the end of the summer, when I arrived with the children, he had run out of original material, but not a single guest complained. In fact, they seemed to enjoy reprisals of his early shows as much as the songs and sketches he borrowed from Vaudeville.

During the day, while Isaac prepared for the shows, or offered dance lessons, or voice, or piano, Ruth and David and I swam in the pool and sunned on the deck and tried our luck at horseshoes and croquet. Isaac was the only one of us who learned tennis, and he had little time for play.

What free time he managed, he gave to the children, which seemed only natural, and right to me. I brought along a bag of books and was content enough to bask in the glory of God's mountainous terrain, and to be thankful for all of my blessings.

AMALIA

We did not see much of each other that first summer, even after Ike and the family returned to Long Island at the end of August. And the first time that we did, it was awkward.

So much of the magic between us lay in our daily contact—knowing each little detail of the other one's day, each reaction to each little detail, keeping current on the events in each other's lives and minds. The rhythm of my weekdays was wound around his morning telephone call, quietly, hurriedly confirming our rendezvous. It included time spent together almost every day. I looked forward to wishing him well at the end of each day, either sharing a drink or another quick call before he went back to Long Island, back to his other life, his real life.

The summer months went by with little contact between us: Only letters I sent—I still lived at home and could not risk receiving mail from Ike there, although he sometimes enclosed a letter for me in Joshua's mail—and the occasional, brief, long distance telephone call, hushed and rushed both because of expense and because of nosy nieces who might enter earshot range at any moment. So much got lost in the crevasse between us that when, at last, we came back together, neither one of us knew where to begin. We were almost like strangers, wanting desperately to express our love, but somehow, forgetting how.

"I missed you," I said over coffee at our spot. We had been coming here nearly a dozen years now. The waitress had aged. I suppose we had, too, though I never noticed it in Ike. The constancy of the smell of stale coffee, no matter what time of day, always comforted me, and the smell of burned toast made me grateful that I had never worked as a waitress, taking the blame for the short-order cook's blunder. In all that time of meeting here, Ike and I had never been caught by anyone we knew. Only the waitress, who still, after all these years, worked the swing shift, might be able to link us as lovers.

It seemed trite to start out saying, "I missed you." But the quiet was uncomfortable and I didn't know what to say to break it.

"I love you." He did not know what to say, either.

We sipped our coffee in nervous silence for a bit, our eyes darting around the run-down room, noticing, after the months away, rips in the orange leatherette upholstery and floor tile corners curling with wear. They must have been there all along. I just never noticed before.

"Think we could do with a bit of privacy?" Ike suggested.

I pushed my cup and saucer away and lay a quarter on the table.

*

Thereafter, we began all our reunions lovemaking. Our bodies instinctively knew what to do even when our tongues had forgotten what to say. Our bodies served as instruments of our love, bringing us close without inhibition, welding our hearts and melding our minds and bridging the time spent apart so completely that after we made love physically, we could pick up the rest of the pieces right where we left off, naturally, comfortably, free of restraint. I would not say that sex was the centerpiece of our love, but perhaps it was the cornerstone: Once in place, all the rest of the pieces fell into place, too.

"Mal, I don't think I can take another summer apart," Ike said in bed when we were through.

"You think you'll go back?"

"They asked me back."

I raised an eyebrow.

"The money's good. The place is nice. The guests, for the most part, are influential families who it couldn't hurt to know. It's not a bad way to spend the summer."

"It sounds as though you've decided, then."

"Well, only on one condition," he said.

"What's that?"

"That you take a job there and spend the summer with me."

"Really?"

"Really. I can't say what the job will be. It could be waiting tables or making beds. Not too glamorous, I know. But at least we'd be together, every day, and every night, for two and a half months."

"Think of it!" I gasped. It was more than I'd ever dreamed of, except the unspoken, impossible dream, the fantasy of being married to Ike.

"But what about Bella, and the children?" My face fell in disappointment. Ike had not thought of everything.

"That's only two weeks at the tail end of the summer. We have plenty of time to think of something. Perhaps you'll catch cold and have to head home. Perhaps I will, preventing their coming up at all. Any number of things could happen by then, and if nothing does, we'll think of something."

"Do you think that they will hire me?"

"I'm pretty sure, if I recommend you. The managers like me, and so did the guests. Shall we try?"

"Yes, let's," I said nuzzling my face to his cheek, brushing my hand across his bare thigh. "Think of it!"

*

And so it was that we spent our summers together, save for the last two weeks, when I faked a debilitating cold that rendered me useless as a housekeeper. Then Ike's family would come up to join him. I know few details of their time at Flagler's. I really didn't want to know. When Ike telephoned home each Sunday at four, I left the room to give him his privacy, I said. But the truth was that I couldn't stand even the thought of hearing him tell another woman, "I love you," even if she was his wife, even if, as he told me, he meant "you" to be plural, as in "I love you *and the children*." Deep down, I knew that in many ways he did love her.

Oh, he never admitted it, never discussed it with me, but it was evident in the little things he did. The regular telephone calls were only part of it. There were other things, too, that I noticed: On trips to the resort canteen, to pick out little gifts or cards for each other, I noticed that he would sometimes buy two items the same. I could only presume that the one I didn't get went to her. But the way that I noticed he loved her the most was in his fierce protection of her. He would not consider not letting her come up at the end of the summer, would not consider having me here when she did, would not do anything that might cause her pain. Even if their passion was limited, and I believe that it was, he loved her in other ways, ways that cemented them together for all time, ways that rendered me illegitimate. He took his commitments seriously, and his marriage commitment was to her.

Deep down, I knew, no matter how much he loved me, Ike would never leave his wife.

BELLA

Maybe I was imagining things, but I felt as though the people at Flagler's this year regarded me in a curious way. It was hard to pinpoint: Was it mockery? pity? compassion? disdain? Neither the guests nor the staff were very friendly toward me during my stay that second summer. In fact, I would characterize them as aloof. They avoided conversation, avoided looking me in the eye. At mealtime, the children and I sat alone at a dining hall table set for ten. No one joined us, and given the lack of warmth in their welcome, I did not sidle up to families already seated, either.

Isaac, too, seemed uneasy when we arrived in mid-August, alternatively doting and dismissive, as though he could not make up his mind about whether he was happy to have us there with him, or whether we were in his way. By day he sometimes left his work aside to take a hike in the woods with us, to swim in a mountain stream or picnic near a waterfall, laughing, enjoying our family life. But that same night, in a show of contempt, he was just as likely to abandon us. I would not find out until he returned the next morning that he had borrowed Mr. Morganstern's motor car to ride into Fallsburgh by himself. Earlier in the summer, under stress from the guests, he said, he had discovered a speakeasy where he could drink until drunk. There was no liquor at Flagler's. None of the mountain resorts served alcohol. They abided by the Prohibition. But the Prohibition did not suppress Isaac. He always was a moody man, a part of his creative nature, I guessed. And so he drank, to lift his spirits. But even after twelve years of marriage, I found his artistic temperament hard to take.

Some days he refused to engage us at all, burying himself in his work, disappearing into the resort's costume room, behind the stage, to the piano, with a sheaf of papers fluttering in his folder as he sped by us in his haste. The children, ages six and ten now, amused themselves with craft projects or kites under the day staff's supervision, and I often was left to myself and to my spiraling inner mind. At the pool, women whispered when I approached. As I neared them they desisted, hid behind sunglasses and magazines, or motioned to a pool boy to bring them a drink in an effort to avert my inquiring eye.

That summer, Isaac's quarters felt somehow homier. Again, it was hard to say just why. The air in the room seemed fresher, more fragrant. Afternoon sun streaming in the window seemed to illuminate an essence of joy. It made me feel giddy. It made me feel warm and safe, and yet, aroused, too. But something told me that I was basking in another's aura. There was something different than last year here, something intangible, some indescribable pleasure that I could sense, but that was not part of me.

As I say, maybe I was imagining things.

AMALIA

"It's not that I'm miserable at home. It's just that I'm miserable without you," Ike said.

I knew precisely how he felt.

My life was livable on its face. I accepted my destiny to become an old maid and made the most of my good fortune to live with my great nieces and nephews, the nearest I expected I would come to having children of my own. I found a job that allowed me to be with them whenever they were home from school. I worked as an assistant to the cook at the public school cafeteria. My single qualification was that I knew *kashrus*, the dietary laws followed by so many of the children in our neighborhood— dietary laws that most of the public school food service staff did not understand or wish to bother to learn, but that, ignored, rendered their meals inedible to many among the student body. I had a roof over my head and enough food to eat. Neither was I miserable at home, but I was growing more and more miserable without Ike.

Against the buoyant backdrop of summer together, coming home provoked great melancholy, hard for both of us to mask, or to shake. Ike covered his by claiming that the High Holy Days depressed him. It was plausible enough: After a summer of skits and stand-up comedy, the Days of Awe were sobering. I could think of no excuse for my own moodiness.

After eight weeks of nights spent together, snippets of sensuality, sneaked and stolen, did not satisfy our insatiable hungers. Might it have been a mistake to allow ourselves unbridled joy? Once we discovered the delights of life shared, life apart, by contrast, was practically unlivable.

The situation was impossible. Again, I considered breaking off our affair. And just as quickly, I knew that by acting on that ill-considered conclusion I would only be punishing myself. How could I cut myself off from my sole source of happiness, the one part of my life that I cherished most?

Stuck is what I was, all right. No matter how I looked at it, no matter what I chose to do, I was the one who wound up the loser.

*

My second summer, which was Ike's third, I didn't have to make beds anymore.

Once the Flagler found out that I knew *kashrus*, and that I worked in a school cafeteria kitchen, they assigned me to the dining hall as an assistant to the chef. In the tradition of the old country, the chef was none other than *Mrs.* Morganstern, the wife of one of the resort owners, the wife of the owner who managed its operations. In the old country, the women ran the businesses to allow the men ample time to pray. Of course, Mr. Morganstern was not in *shul*. In this, the industrial age in the United States, he fancied himself a captain of commerce. More likely, he was captain of Flagler's tennis team. But tradition is tradition, as I knew all too well.

Mrs. Morganstern was a cheapskate if I ever knew one, which probably was why the place made so much money. She scrimped wherever she could get away with it, skimming a tablespoon of whipping cream from a recipe to refill the creamers on the tables, usually half with cream and half with milk, or shorting a cake by an egg or two that she'd hold over for the next morning's breakfast. Yet, surprisingly to me, no one complained about the food. And I had to admit, even to myself, the quality of the food was good.

I made the mistake, one day in the kitchen, of calling attention to Mrs. Morganstern's systematic frugality.

I stood, in my rumpled, jelly-stained apron, holding the industrial mixer steady, while Mrs. Morganstern, in a dark street-length dress, paced back and forth from ice box to bowl, adding butter and eggs, sugar and cocoa, flour, vanilla, baking soda and salt. Her recipe stand stood facing me, and I could see, as I had noticed a dozen times before, that where the mess-sized brownie recipe called for twelve eggs, she cracked ten; that where six cups of flour were required, she dumped in only four-and-a-half.

"Mrs. Morganstern," I called, over the whir of the mixing machine, "The recipe calls for twelve eggs. You're short."

"Never mind, Dear," she said, ignoring my observation.

"I think you need a bit more flour," I called out as she emptied the measuring cup into the bowl. I stood back as the flour dust blew around the white tile room.

And so it went, until finally, she finished adding ingredients and the silky-rich smell of chocolate crept into the kitchen even before the cookie tins of smooth brown batter were set to baking in the ovens.

Now, in the comparative quiet of the idle kitchen, Mrs. Morganstern addressed my query.

"Mal," she advised me familiarly. "There's one lesson you ought to learn in my kitchen, and it isn't how to cook. It's simply this: It's no trick to take a diamond and make it look like a diamond. The trick is to make glass sparkle like a rare gem."

BELLA

I had just about lost my patience with Isaac's late night calls, about early appointments and the need to stay the night in town.

"Honestly," I complained to my sister. "The children miss Isaac so terribly, and, of course, I am dreadfully lonely, too. If only it was not such a long way, if only I had found a place in town."

My sad reality was that I could not bring my man home, that some greater lure held him in the city, away from the children, away from me, but I would never disclose such a personal grievance, not even to my sister, who I adored and told my other secrets to.

"Funny that you should mention that now," Lilly answered over the telephone. I rarely got into town myself and was happy that we both had telephones. "The family who lives below us just moved out to a house in the suburbs, so the flat is vacant. Are you interested?"

"Am I?" I asked.

"Well, you know the neighborhood. Scandinavian. Nice. And you know my apartment. The one downstairs is the same. It is spacious enough, though certainly not a palace. But, as you say, the proximity to the places that Isaac works is an amenity unavailable on Long Island."

"Right," I agreed. "And how wonderful it would be to be so near you! Oh, Lilly, it would be like living at home again!"

"It would. Yes, it would be awfully nice to have you nearby. Would you like me to ask the landlord to hold it, just until you and Isaac can decide?"

"Well, what could it hurt?" I conceded, my ambivalence detectable in my tone.

Amalia was back in his life, I could not deny knowing. But how could I know whether moving to town would prove to be to my advantage, or hers?

*

It was almost summer, and for the first time in five years, Isaac had not signed on to work at Flagler's. We would spend our summer in town.

With the children growing older—now thirteen and nine—I was less and less able to occupy them at home through the interminable void known as summer vacation. In previous years, we had, at least, looked forward to our two weeks in the Catskills. But with Isaac surrendering his employee status, we had to forfeit our holiday there. We could not afford to pay full freight at Flagler's.

Ruth and David needed more to do than play stickball or kick the can with the children in our new, Brooklyn Heights neighborhood. Ruth was fast outgrowing children's games and fast approaching womanhood. David might have been satisfied, but for the fact that his sister was not. Whatever Ruth wanted to do, David wanted to do, too.

So I began to inquire about sleep-away camps. The synagogue consortium ran quite a few, and so I called on Isaac's brother—Uncle Israel, I called him, because the children did, and because it felt strange to call a rabbi, even a rabbi who is also my brother-in-law, by his first name—to ask his advice on the various youth programs. Even though he was orthodox, as we were, he was the senior rabbi at the conservative, Kane Street Synagogue, to which we had returned when we moved back to Brooklyn.

"Of course, we must have a camp that keeps a kosher kitchen," I told him. "And one that strictly observes *Shabbos*."

"Yes, yes, naturally," Uncle Israel said. "But beyond that, what are you looking for?"

"Well, something recreational, I suppose, though Ruth really loves to read, so there should be some quiet time for her to do so, and someplace pretty, with lots of trees and small forest animals."

"A real camp experience, eh?" asked Israel.

"And a focus on music," I went on. "Music is so important to our family, I would hate to send them somewhere without it."

"Mmmm hmmm," he was jotting down some notes now. "How long a stay were you thinking of, Bella?"

"Well, two or three weeks, I suppose, though we would have to consider the cost. I have been saving a little bit each month, but our resources, as you know, are not vast."

"Mmmm hmmm," he said. "Well, I know a lovely camp in the Catskills. Let me find out about fees and get back to you, eh?"

"Oh, Uncle Israel, you are always so helpful to me."

"Love to the children," he kissed me lightly on the cheek and walked me to his office door.

*

I reported the visit to Isaac that night.

"Summer camp would be wonderful for the children," he said, strangely detached from his own words. "Pursue it, Bella, whatever the cost."

*

Isaac seemed distant, distracted, intent on something he would not disclose. His melancholy did not surprise me; I had seen it so many times before. But usually, he was downcast in the darker months of fall and winter, his gloom lifting with the cloud cover and the onset of spring. This last winter had produced only a mild moodswing in Isaac. But now, though I expected his upbeat persona to return as spring began to turn to summer, his depression persisted. He was lost in thought. I had to repeat everything I told him. He never heard me the first time I spoke, always too distracted to pick up that someone was speaking to him until the words had already wafted by.

The children did not seem to notice, but they were so preoccupied with their own busy lives—their studies, their friends, and now, the *bar mitz-vah* parties thrown for each of the boys in Ruth's class—that they had little time, let alone inclination, to examine their father's detached behavior.

I tried to insulate myself. I sewed beautiful party dresses for Ruth to wear to each weekend affair, and sometimes sewed matching knickers and blazers for David, though he did not like to dress like his sister much anymore. I involved myself in the children's classroom projects, and I took on a new volunteer job, refinishing the clothing donated to our local Jewish resale shop with the proceeds going to feed and clothe the poor. I rejoined the book group at the synagogue. I had missed reading during our year away, and missed the intellectual exchange when I found myself segregated in suburban Long Island.

My conversation with Isaac was limited to reports on my day and the children's. He told little of his pursuits, and I did not press for information. Perhaps I was afraid of what I would hear.

And then, one night after the children were asleep, my very worst nightmare came to pass.

*

It was a typical night in our household. We had finished our dinner and cleaned up the dishes. The children were bathed and tucked in to bed, and, as was so often our custom, Isaac sat in his armchair reading the *Forvitz*, while I sat in my straight-backed chair at the table, reading my book group's selection for the month.

"Bella?"

"Hmmmm?" I did not look up from the page.

"Bella," he said. "I am so sorry," his voice dropped low and flat, emotionless. "You are a lovely woman, Bella. He paused. He gulped. He could hardly get his words out. "You are, but, but…

"I am afraid that I do not love you."

Silence.

And then, "I feel that I have no choice but to leave."

I could not believe my ears! I must be imagining! I looked up. I looked hard.

"What are you saying?" I demanded.

"I do not wish to cause a scene. I will leave when the children are away at camp. When they return you can tell them that I am away, on business."

"You have this all planned out, have you?" I accused him, my fury fast rising to the surface.

"Yes, Bella. I have."

"Isaac," I backed off. I softened. "You need not make any major decision tonight." My heart was racing. I tried to sound rational. "Give this some time. You could grow to love me. What is love, anyway? You must think of the children…And your position in the community." I did not ask him to think of me.

"I have thought. For years, I have thought, Bella. And I have decided, not quickly. Not easily. But over time. We will manage until the children go. Then I will go, and leave you in peace.

"Good night, Bella."

He walked into the bedroom and closed the door.

*

How could the children ever have guessed that these good-bye kisses would be their last? I could not choke back the tears as I watched. He hugged them extra tight to his breast. He looked each of them deep in the eye. He told them how very much he loved them, how proud he was of each of them, how he wished for them the best time ever. He swallowed his tears until they boarded their bus, bound for two weeks of summer fun, never suspecting that upon their return they would find their world turned upside down.

Isaac stepped back next to me, surrounded by cheering, waving parents each trying to catch their own children's eyes. We joined in, too, and as we called our good-byes to our little ones, I wondered how Isaac could bring himself to leave them. They were so precious, so innocent of any unfairness, any ills that could cross their paths to adulthood.

The bus pulled away from the teeming crowd, and I turned to focus my gaze on Isaac. He was engrossed in watching our children depart, seated one behind the other in window seats, sharing the benches with their respective best friends. It was as if he was trying to memorize their faces, their gestures, their enthusiastic anticipation of their first time at sleep-away camp.

"Isaac?" I uttered his name as if it were a question.

His tentative smile turned stern.

"Let's go home," he said.

*

I awakened to the sound of keys jangling in a pants pocket, and the clink of a metal belt buckle closing.

He really is going, I thought in the softness of our marriage bed.

"Wait a minute, Mister!" I wanted to shout. "You cannot go! I have been patient, extremely patient with you until now. I have endured the embarrassment of your infidelity, carrying myself as respectably as I could while the entire community knew the truth. I have swallowed my pride as you headed out at least one, sometimes more, nights every week. I have opened my home to a collection of friends and relations who show me no respect, not that they should, the way they see you treat me…"

But even as I raged against him, I could not speak the words aloud. Even as fifteen years of raw emotion invisibly splashed and smashed the bedroom walls, even as I finally, righteously expressed my true thoughts—though only expressed them to myself—even as I defiantly, triumphantly, distilled what I had been feeling since we met at the altar all those years ago, he cut me off mid-stream, swung round to my side of the bed, and, just as the knock came at the door, gave me a quick peck on the cheek, picked up his bag, and left the house.

That was the last time that I saw Isaac.

Four months later the stock market crashed, triggering a decline in the American economy that would come to be known as the Great Depression.

It was a depression from which I would never recover.

*

I used his own excuse with Ruth and David, told them that Poppy had gone out west, on business, and that he would be back before we knew it. I told them how sorry he was that he could not tell them good-bye himself, and described how he wanted to kiss them and tell them that he loved

them, but that we would all be together again soon enough. I hated to lie
to my own children, but how else could I explain Isaac's disappearance
without their feeling abandoned by him?

"Will Poppy be back for my birthday?" asked David.

His birthday was a full month away, but already he had begun to antic-
ipate it, talking about friends to invite and what they would do and, of
course, speculating on the gifts he might get.

"He would not miss it, Sweetheart," I assured him, fighting back tears of
sorrow, and of rage. "He will be back way before your birthday. He will
probably bring you an extra special present just for big boys, ten and older."

I looked at Ruth. She looked forlorn.

"I am sure they have lots of pretty things for thirteen-year-old girls
where Poppy is, too," I told her. "Have you ever known Poppy to forget
you when it comes to presents? You are his very special girl."

That perked her up right away, and I hoped to God that Isaac would
come through. Whatever other faults he had, he always had been a good
father to our two. So I presumed that he would not let them down.

Otherwise, they took the news rather well.

They went about their regular routines, school and homework and
friends and *shul*, but never forgetting, always missing their father, and
each day wondering, 'How many tomorrows till Poppy comes home?'
And each day I assured them that he would be home soon, sooner than
they even knew, and that once he was home we would have a big celebration with lots of cousins and uncles and aunts, and lots of good food and
music and games.

Day after day I awaited a letter.

Day after day, I heard not a word.

Thirty days, thirty-one days, thirty-two, and not so much as a card in
the post. Well, I reasoned, it would take a card as long to get here as it
would take Isaac to bring it here himself. A letter will come for the children any day now, I am sure of it. It must be soon. For the sake of the
children. Word will come soon.

And then, finally, a letter came, but not for the children. It was addressed to me. This letter:

November 16, 1929

Dear Bella,

I doubt that you can ever forgive me, not so much for leaving as for never really being there. I regret that even in fifteen years' time, I did not reveal to you the man I am. By now you must know I am passionate to a fault—not only for music, but for the stirrings of the heart. Truly, I tried to ignore that fatal flaw; I never wanted to hurt any of you. I tried, to the best of my ability, to fulfill my obligation to you, to be your faithful, loving husband, to shower you with all the affection that poured, misdirected, from this poor soul.

I have obtained a civil divorce, a copy of which I have wired to your brother-in-law, who, no doubt, will offer you legal counsel. I hope that you will allow me the time to resettle my own affairs before we get to the matter of the *get*. I assure you that I expect nothing from you; in fact, I have instructed my brother, Israel, to forward my share of any royalties from our jointly published compositions to you. I know of nothing else I have of value; if you do, you have only to say so and it is yours.

As to what to tell the children, I hope to be in touch with them, to write, to call and to visit them, with your permission, of course. I hope that with time you will find a way to explain to them that what happened between us was no one's fault: Not either of theirs, and certainly not yours. Perhaps we all were victims of a cruel fate, an accident, an accident of love.

I do not intend to plague you with reminders of myself. Instead, I will step aside with the sincerest hope that soon you, too, will be able to make a new life.

As always,

Isaac E. Grossman

I crunched the paper inside my fist. I pounded the kitchen table. I gasped, then wailed like a cow in labor. Thank goodness the children were off at school. I had started to believe the lie I told them. But now, this letter was tangible evidence of the truth: Isaac was not ever coming back. Not to me. Not to them. What was going to become of them? What was going to become of me? What to do? What to do? What to do?

I buried my face in my hands, smudging the ink on Isaac's letter with my tears.

The nightmare was over. Isaac was dead to me now. I was so overwhelmed by the enormity of the implications—the decisions to make, the directions to take—yet only one thought plagued my mind right then: What to tell David about his birthday?

AMALIA

The problem with having an illicit affair is that there's no one to talk to about your lover.

It never occurred to me, at least lately, that Ike would walk out on me again.

Ike and I, we were like clockwork: We shared our mornings, whenever and wherever we could, and went out at least a few evenings a week after the movie show.

But it had been three days since I'd heard from Ike; already I was dreading my breakfast at the coffee shop where I took my morning meal each day, and the emptiness that grew inside me as I placed my order, and no Ike; read the paper, and no Ike; picked at my food, and no Ike; as I finished my last bite of toast, lingered over my last cup of coffee, glanced frequently, hopefully over the top of my newspaper, out the window, and still, no Ike arrived to steal me away to an hour, or two, or three, of heaven.

He often met me after he worked the movie show, at a little bar down the street from the cinema. Many of our acquaintances drank there; most of them single, most detached from the traditions of the community our parents had built on New York's Lower East Side. They were the secularized, second generation. They didn't ask questions, we didn't offer explanations, and even if they guessed the truth, I doubt very much that they would have cared. They were good company, and I enjoyed a nightcap with them before bed. I enjoyed it even more when Ike managed to join me, which he did two or three times a week. Since he couldn't call for me at home, where my family would be shamed by my unscrupulous behavior, we had our set meeting places, and rarely, rarely failed to hook up as planned.

Days ticked by without a word, and I had the nagging sense that something was terribly, terribly wrong: What could have become of Ike?

BELLA

I could hardly believe my eyes when my brother-in-law, Meyer, presented the document that Isaac had delivered to him by registered mail: A decree of divorcement by authority of the State of Nevada.

"Bella H. Grossman, plaintiff
vs.
Isaac E. Grossman, defendant
The Hon. Emmett J. Reynolds, presiding
Judgment Index No. 379/26

The above entitled action having been duly brought by the plaintiff for a judgment of absolute divorce in favor of the plaintiff and against the defendant dissolving the marriage rela- tion heretofore existing between the parties hereto by reason of the plaintiff and defendant having lived separate and apart for a period of six months or more, and the summons and verified complaint bearing the notation "Action for a Divorce" having been duly personally served upon the defendant within the State of Nevada, and the defendant not having appeared within the statutory period prescribed therefor, and his time to do so having fully expired, and plaintiff having applied to this Court for judgment for the relief demanded in the complaint, and having presented her verified complaint and written proof of the service of the summons and verified complaint upon the defendant, and the defendant not having appeared upon such application, and testimony having been given in open Court on the 16th day of December, 1929, before me, satisfactorily proving the allegations of the verified complaint, and having heard and considered the proof offered and having made a decision in writing stating separately the facts found and the conclusions of law and upon written proof that the defendant is not in the military service of the United States of America;

NOW, on motion of Bella H. Grossman, plaintiff, it is

ORDERED, ADJUDGED AND DECREED that the plaintiff be and hereby is granted judgment dissolving the marriage relation heretofore existing between Bella H. Grossman, plaintiff, and Isaac E. Grossman, defendant, by reason of the plaintiff and defendant having lived separate and apart for a period of six months or more."

*

I put down the paper and looked up, blankly, at Meyer.

"For the legal record, you are the victor, the spouse who petitioned for this divorce," Meyer began to explain.

Meyer could not argue that Isaac's was anything but a clever ploy. Not only was I deemed the winner—a status that might ease my transition from married to single in our society—but by making himself the defendant, Isaac could arrange for all the papers to be served on himself. By not responding to them, he retained the power to expedite the legal process he had set in motion. Isaac had thought of everything—or had hired a lawyer who thought of everything, Meyer noted.

Of course, such a document did not free me by my standards. I would need a *get*—a Jewish divorce—in order to get on with my life. But what did I want of another husband? One experience had been enough for me. I had my children. I had my home. And I still had my self-respect. I was neither in need nor in want of a step-father interfering in my children's upbringing, telling me what and what not to do, making a fool of me the way Isaac had done.

In my mind, Isaac may as well have been dead.

So that is the way I decided to tell it.

I became the widow Bella Grossman. I would report that Isaac had suffered a fatal accident out West.

The only impediment to the story was Isaac's wish to correspond with the children. Though I hated him for what he had done to them, I believed in my heart that they would be better served by a father who cared—even from afar—than from no father at all. The price they would pay for Isaac's correspondence would be to keep the family's secret.

AMALIA

I had never left New York City before.

I spent the days leading up to my leaving casing the marketplace for cheap, but presentable travel clothes. I didn't want to spend all the money that Ike sent me when he finally wired me to come West. You never know when you might need spare cash, especially when you don't know where or how you might come by some more. It never occurred to me to consider what I would wear once I got there. But then, I didn't imagine we'd stay in Los Angeles, only meet there and make our way—where? I hadn't thought very far ahead. I was motivated only by the short-term—by reconnecting with Ike—and didn't consider longer-term consequences: Consequences like where we would live, where he would work, how we could make it in an inhospitable, unknown frontier where the rules we lived by were null and void.

Null and void.

Ike's marriage, now, was null and void, maybe not by Jewish law, but certainly by the law of the land.

I could hardly imagine what it would be like to stroll hand-in-hand in public view, to kiss him with passion on our first encounter, to be able to go to public places—restaurants, theaters, movie shows—and to display our affection openly, without each of us keeping one eye pointed over the other's shoulder to see if someone we knew was nearby.

Yet I was also gripped by fear. What if I got there and Ike was not there? What if he was there, but could not find work? What if we could not find a place? The what-ifs plagued me, and the negative side of this proposition sucked me into a downward spiral. Maybe I had better not go. Maybe, as much as I wanted him, needed him, loved him with all my heart, I, and he, too, ultimately, would be better off to live the lives that our families had planned for us, and to forgo the opportunity fate had handed to us. The disappointment weighed on me, and I felt my shoulders slouch in defeat.

Eeeeeeeeeeee!

The steaming tea pot commanded my attention, snapping me back to the here and now, reminding me of the very short-term task that I had left for last: Telling my family that I was leaving. I had waited to tell them intentionally, to allow myself the possibility of changing my mind. Once I told them I was leaving, I could never return. I prayed I would make the right decision, because, once made, there was no turning back. No, if I stayed I would lose Ike forever, for he could never return to this place, and I would surely lose track of his whereabouts. And if I went, there could be no running back home, no warm, safe place where everything could be all right again if things didn't go according to plan.

No, if things didn't work out, nothing would be all right again, ever.

I knew that they would disapprove, that they would scowl and scold and try to scorn me out of leaving; that they would capitalize on my sense of duty to family, on my indebtedness to them for all the years of kindness they had shown me when they were under no obligation to do so; on my selfless view of myself, convincing me that even so much as contemplating what I intended to carry out was an act of pure and utter selfishness.

On the other hand, what had I to lose?

I made my tea and walked upstairs, still wavering on what to do. I opened my door, and in a flash, I knew: For the first time in years, my eyes alit on the yellowed ballet slippers suspended from their rusty nail in the cracked bedroom wall.

At last, I had been asked to dance.

I had prayed my whole life for this invitation. No matter the risks, I would not forgo it.

*

"I have some news," I announced at dinner.

Something in my voice must have commanded their attention, because all forks stopped shoveling—a rare moment at our table. All glasses stopped tinkling. All conversation stopped. All eyes were on me.

"So, *nu*, Amalia? What kind of news merits such a heralding?" My niece Gert's husband, Max, condescended. He had always been a sarcastic fellow, and I doubt very much that Gert loved this man. Alas, such a marriage was not so out of the ordinary for our time, and for this place.

I swallowed hard. I decided to put my decision in the best light possible, or, at least, a positive light as far as they were concerned.

"I'm going to be married," I said, rather jittery.

"Married! *Mazel tov! Baruch hashem!*" Gert expressed the usual best wishes. "And I don't need to ask who the bridegroom will be..."

There was a solicitous lilt in her voice, as if adding, "Do I?" and a glance at Max as if to say, "A nice Jewish doctor. How about that?" She raised an eyebrow at me, asking silently, hopefully, for confirmation that I would marry Joshua.

Uh oh. I hadn't anticipated their making assumptions. But it was only natural for them to assume that I would marry the man who they thought had been courting me.

"I know he's an untraditional sort, Mal," Max challenged me, his elbows on the table, his mouth still half full of food. "I can't really say that I'm surprised that he failed to even go through the motions, for tradition's sake if nothing else, of asking for your hand in marriage. But," he stared down from the head of the table at me, "Where is Joshua tonight? Shouldn't he be here for such an announcement?"

"Yes, yes," Rose chimed in. "Where is Joshua? Why isn't he here to celebrate the happy news, Mal?"

Querying eyes focused on me from all sides, and I was too flustered to look back at them. I stared down at my plate. I could hardly speak, so I whispered.

"It's not Joshua," I said.

"What?" Rose's husband bellowed now. "Who? Amalia, I don't think that I heard you right."

"Yes." I stuttered, my face still in the plate. "You heard me right. It isn't Joshua. The 'lucky' bridegroom, such as he is, is Ike. Ike Grossman."

Their four faces flushed deep crimson. They glanced nervously at one another, wondering, I suppose, what to say, hoping that some one among them would say something to make the awkward moment pass. Questions shot out from their eyes, if not their mouths, and my cheeks flushed, too, as I anticipated, and addressed them.

"Ike went to Reno, Nevada," I started. "He got a divorce. He sent me a telegram, along with some money, asking me to come to him in Los Angeles, and to marry him.

"It should come as no surprise to you all, though I suppose in your own way, you were trying to protect me—and yourselves—by looking the other way when our illicit courtship treaded too close to home. But you had to have known, didn't you, that Ike and I never stopped seeing each other, never stopped loving each other, never stopped dreaming of a time when we could be together?"

I paused, waiting for the maelstrom of sniping that surely would follow, the angry voices forbidding me from following my heart, railing against my betrayal of the family, my shameful disregard for the family name.

But instead, my news was met with something I wouldn't have anticipated: Stone, cold silence.

"I'll be leaving tomorrow," I said quietly.

"Good riddance," Max murmured.

I pushed my chair away from the table.

"Excuse me," I mumbled.

I bit the insides of my cheeks. I swallowed hard. I refused to give them the satisfaction. And somehow, in that moment, I knew that I had decided it right. It took all of my self-control to choke back the tears until I got to my room.

*

No one wished me well on my way.

I left the house early, before the others were up. I left my key on the kitchen counter. When I pulled the door shut and heard the lock click into place, I knew that I could never come back home.

Now, I carried home in my heart.

I bundled myself in my warmest coat, a hand-me-down that smelled of mothballs; I wrapped my head in a woolen scarf. In my hand I grasped a battered suitcase that I had found in my sister's attic. It looked as though it had many miles on it, as though it had been through plenty already: Probably it came from the old country. It was blue and round, about twenty-four inches in diameter, and though it held not an awful lot, it would have to do as a carrying case for all the worldly goods I would take with me into my new life: A skirt, a blouse, some underwear, a change of shoes, a photograph of my mother, my toiletries, some toilet water, and yes, I had to squeeze them in: I couldn't leave my ballet slippers.

I trudged the three miles from the house to the train station, awaiting the seven-thirteen heading west.

Few other travelers stood on the platform: A well-dressed woman holding a small child by his mitten; a businessman with a briefcase in hand; a blind man clutching a leash attached to his German-shepherd seeing-eye dog.

When I settled into my seat on board, I realized that I was terribly hungry. After the abrupt end to the meal last night, I'd been up most of the night sorting through the debris that decorated the first thirty years of my life, trying to decide what to keep and what I could bear to leave behind. I felt unwelcome to help myself to breakfast, after Max's abrasive final words. No wonder I'd worked up an appetite.

I opened my tote bag and reached for an apple.

Its loud crunch drew the attention of the others in the cabin with me. Disapproving glances fell my way, and yet, somehow, I didn't care anymore. I had suffered disapproving glances for as long as I could remember, and now, I hoped, I prayed, things were finally going to work out my way, in spite of all the nay-sayers, in spite of the censure of society. I enjoyed my apple. I relished its crisp crunch. I sat back and smiled, snidely, I admit, at those who consigned their condemnation on me.

*

I didn't sleep well on the train.

I'd decided against taking a berth by night: It was an extra expense, after all, and what did I need with extravagance? The one luxury I had allowed myself was a silk peignoir, cut low and lacy, brushing the curve of my breast in the front, and brushing the curve of my knee in back. But except for this one concession to romance, Ike and I would have to watch our pennies if we were to make it through this transition intact.

My clothes were rumpled by the end of the second day of travel; black circles formed beneath my eyes, and I felt like the child in the back seat of a motor car, asking, always asking, "Aren't we there yet?"

But for my exhaustion and my newfound, brazen, what-do-I-care attitude, the trip across country was unremarkable. Various folk shuffled in and out of my cabin, hardly taking notice of me, though I tried to memorize each of their faces. This trip was one to be retold, I day-dreamed, alternating my glances into strange faces with glances out the plate glass picture window onto mile after mile of empty, open field. There wasn't much to this western frontier. I began to wonder what I would find at my final destination. I wondered whether there were stores out there, whether there were apartment houses, marketplaces, synagogues, the comforts that I had come to expect of life.

I wondered whether Ike had received the hasty word I'd wired off: "ON MY WAY. stop. DPT 1/10 @ 7 AM. stop. ILY2, A."

The train bumped along, and my body ached from my own lack of movement, too exhausted, too excited, to fall asleep.

I hoped that Ike would be at the other end.

If he weren't, I'd be at a loss for what to do next. I hadn't the money to stay on by myself, and while I had set aside enough to get me back to New York, those I knew there were by now already sitting *shiva* for me.

I placed my right hand over my left breast, to ensure that my money was still tucked snugly in place, inside the left cup of my brassiere.

Three more days to go.

I settled back, closed my eyes, and for the umpteenth time, I tried, without success, to sleep.

*

I searched the faces in the crowd when my train pulled in to Los Angeles. I pressed my face against the glass as the train slowly, slowly, braked to a stop. My, but people looked different here: Many men wore light suits, and even by day, the women were dolled up, in short, beaded dresses with shoulder wraps, their bobbed heads bouncing about smiling faces, their jewelry glistening in the sun. They looked like they were dressed for a party; they acted like partygoers, too—laughing, pointing, squealing as one by one, each identified the people they had come to meet.

I looked at my own attire with dismay, so prudently selected just a few days ago and yet, in this context, so out of place. I felt dowdy by comparison in my black traveling suit, buttoned from my waist to the top of my neck, my heavy dark skirt, deeply creased, falling in folds to my ankles. Yet I was no older, and certainly no more prudish than any of the women whose made-up eyes looked back through the train windows at me.

The crowd dispersed into huddles, hovering around the doors at the ends of each rail car. Still, I searched the faces, and still, as groups of friends peeled off the platform and on into town, I recognized no one in this place.

I retrieved my valise and my tote bag from the storage bin beneath my seat, smoothed my waistcoat over my hips and got off the train, one of the last to alight.

I stood on the platform a few moments more, looking over my shoulder, this way and that, as if I expected Ike to appear there at any moment.

He didn't.

When my train steamed back out of the station, I picked up my bag and turned toward the street.

*

I was rumpled and hot, overdressed for the West, as I boarded the bus that would take me downtown. Alone and, I admit, afraid, I knew the name of only one place here—the place where I'd sent my telegram.

"Would you mind telling me where to transfer for Pasadena?" I asked the bus driver as I sat down behind him.

My dress told him I was not from here.

"You got it, Sweetheart," he answered me.

It was a short ride downtown, where most of the buildings housed offices. Broad, well-swept sidewalks bathed in sunlight served as a walkway for the fancy folk migrating from place to place. Billboards that I expected would light up at night screamed out the names of the latest movie releases. A block and a half up, I saw the bus depot.

"This is your stop, Sweetheart," the driver said, pointing. "Just ask inside for the northbound bus to Pasadena."

I stepped out into the sun, depleted and sticky all over with sweat, my hair afrizz, my clothes smelling of diesel fuel. Though I traveled light, my bags felt heavy to my weary body, and I straddled a bench to collect myself. The bus I got off belched a billow of exhaust on me as it pulled out of the depot, into mid-day traffic.

I coughed.

I sighed.

I had made it all this way, only to discover that Ike was not here.

A wave of loneliness washed over me, and a sense of dread, and of fear, crept into my heart. I was spent, emotionally and physically. I had run out of food a day and a half ago, and didn't want to spend my money needlessly: My only activity had been sitting on the train; I figured I needed no energy for that. I trembled, both from hunger and nerves, not to mention sheer exhaustion. I couldn't think of what to do next, couldn't figure out where to go, and finally, I gave in to my despair. I dropped my face in my hands and bawled.

*

Oh my God. God help me. Oh my God. God help me.

I was snatched from collapse by someone too close, someone straddling the bench behind me, panting unwelcome, hot breath on the nape of my neck.

My heart raced.

My pulse soared.

Panic.

Oh my God. God help me. Oh my God. God help me.

With fervor I would have thought was all drained out of me, I whipped my tote around my body to smack the assailant away from me, but he blocked my bag with his forearm.

Oh my God. Oh my God. Oh my...

Tension spit from my every pore. Adrenaline tore me free from his hold. I turned, poised to run, when I saw my attacker's face: Ike smiled broadly, flirtatiously.

"Oh my God! Oh, thank God!"

I was relieved and furious at the same time.

I beat my fists against his chest as he reached to clasp protective hands around my waist, like a parent offering security, through embrace, to a child in the midst of a temper tantrum.

"You frightened me so! I thought you were a thief, a thug, a ruffian, a, a, I don't know what! Don't ever, ever..."

My open palms slapped at his chest now, sapping my last little bit of strength until, finally, I had to stop, to rest.

"I'm sorry, Honey. I only meant it in fun." He leaned back to look at me as he spoke.

"God, it's good to see you," he sighed.

"Good Lord, Ike! In fun? You scared the life out of me! My heart is racing from fright!"

"I'm sorry, Baby," he said, truly remorseful now. "I didn't mean it. Honestly. I never want to frighten you."

He pulled me close and held me gently.

"You're in safe hands now, Mal. You always will be."

He picked up my bags and, wrapping his arm about my shoulders, steered me across the street to a waiting motor car.

*

My travel-worn body was feather-light in Ike's arms. My head drooped against his shoulder; my legs dangled over the crook of his elbow. He carried me, like a baby, up the hotel elevator, down the hallway, into the room he was calling home. I hadn't realized quite how tension-wracked I had been until Ike laid me, gently, on the bed: I exhaled strain like a dragon blows fire, in slow, steady breaths that rendered me, finally, released.

"That's right. Relax," he whispered. "Close your eyes. Let me tend you."

One by one, he pulled off my boots, pausing to caress each aching, hot foot as if it were a precious thing. He lifted my skirt to release each garter, stroking each tired leg as he smoothed my stockings down, over, and off. He loosened the buckles at my waist, allowing my skirt to slip to the floor when he tugged its hem from the foot of the bed. He unbuttoned my waistcoat. Fresh air bathed me, finally, in cool relief. Agile fingers released the snaps, hooks, and ties of my undergarments, which, once loosened, easily fell away, freeing my frame for the first time in days. I lay limp and silent, approaching slumber.

The soothing sound of rushing water filled my head as I drifted there, on the cusp between wakefulness and sleep, uncertain whether I was dreaming, or whether, truly, I was home, at last.

Strong arms scooped me up again, then lowered me into a tepid bath. His wide palm cradled my heavy head; his loving hand ladled lukewarm water over my loose hair. His fingertips traced soap circles over my scalp, massaging my head in mild, fragrant shampoo, then worked their way down to sketch the same rings on my brow, on my temples, between my eyes, over my cheeks, along my jaw bone, and all the while, warm wavelets licked at my collarbone and breast, bobbing, breaking the water's smooth surface.

"You're so beautiful," he whispered, as if to himself.

His firm palm caressed my belly, inching down, between my legs to gently wash my woman-parts, then worked down further, to my thighs, my calves, my feet, between the toes, to my very soles.

I floated. Let me dream a little longer, my mind whispered to me. Let me believe, for a moment, that I might be fulfilled, at last.

Some restful minutes later—just how many, I couldn't say—I felt myself lifted from the tub, the plip-plip-plip of driplets off my body splashing the water beneath, like so many raindrops pelting a pond. Strong arms wrapped me in terry cloth, patted me dry, toweled my hair and wrapped it up like a turban.

He carried me to the bed again, where he laid me, face down, and began pressing his fingertips into my flesh: Deep, muscle work over my tired shoulders and neck, down naked arms to the backs of my hands, then over the other side, to my palms, and back up the undersides of my upper limbs, turning me over as he worked. With each touch I melted, deeper, into the mattress, into the dream.

He blew long, cool breaths over my exposed skin as he continued caressing me, working the muscles of my legs, down the outside, up the inside—pausing to pet my soft femininity, fondling, exploring, stroking, teasing—then down the inside of my other thigh, up the outside, and back again, until, to my own surprise, I flushed in fiery passion, despite my depletion, my exhaustion.

Slowly, he loosened my towel from its hitching place at my bosom. His gaze warmed my naked body to a rosy glow. I arched toward him, wrapping my arms around his neck, wrapping my legs around his waist, thrusting involuntarily. He spread his fingers between each of my ribs, and set his thumbs beneath my breasts, pushing up, then brushing his fingers over curved, round mounds until his hands came to rest upon my heart.

For a moment, we were utterly still. The only sound in the room was our breath, deep and steady, as our eyes locked on one another.

I shuddered.

"Shhhhhhhh," he whispered, cradling me close.

He pulled back the bed covers and wedged me between the cool, crisply pressed sheets.

"Sleep, my angel." He stroked my hair. "I'll be right here."

*

Some hours later, I awoke. Ike lay beside me, asleep, in his now-rumpled suit.

"He sleeps," I whispered, grazing his hand with my fingertips to test whether I was dreaming or not.

My touch triggered a stretch, and a loud breath. Then he rolled to his side and continued his slumber. It occurred to me then, that I had never seen Ike completely at rest.

I snuggled back under the covers. I stared at the ceiling. I wondered what time it was. The train trip had thrown off my timing entirely. My best guess was that it was after midnight. My stomach growled. How long was it since I had eaten?

I gazed fondly at Ike, whose attempt at humor had scared me so, whose quick retreat to gentle guardian had nurtured me to bath, to bed, to sleep and to dream.

I stroked the curve of his hip, then slid across the bed to peer over his shoulder at his cheek, stubbly now from these night hours' growth. I kissed him softly there. His eyes batted, blinked, then turned to beseech me.

"Mal," he said, still half asleep. "Forgive me?"

I nodded.

He rolled to his back and I straddled him, leaning forward to taste our first kiss. His lips felt full and firm on mine, and I let them guide my mouth open, round, let his tongue trace the inside of my lips.

Slowly, I rocked back on my hips, dropped my hands to massage his chest, and nimbly opened his shirt buttons. He reached up to pinch my soft, full, breasts, still pink as newborn mice from the bath. His fingers trickled across me as if they were stroking piano keys.

"Too much clothes," I whispered, unknotting his loosened tie.

"Way too much," he whispered back.

His broad, bare chest felt warm to my hands when I peeled his shirt back and pushed it aside. I dropped forward again, dusting my own chest across his, and intermittently pulling just far enough away to leave his flesh hungry, his eyes imploring me for more. I scooted back, now straddling his thighs, making his trouser tops accessible.

How I had missed his hands on my body! I tossed back my head and stroked my own front, from my collarbone, down, lingering on my breasts, then smoothing over my belly and hips before I opened his pants.

I pulled his trousers with me as I scooted back even further, to the bed's edge. Then I climbed back on top, lying forehead to forehead, nose to nose with the one person who meant everything to me, the only person in my life now.

I lifted my hips to catch him in the space between my legs.

We melted into one.

And it was very good.

*

I always whispered when we made love, a throwback, perhaps, to our days in hiding, when we never knew who might be lurking, listening in the next apartment, in the next room, or even—dare I admit it?—in the bushes.

Pasadena was a honeymoon. We strolled, we sunned, we slept until noon. We made love whenever we wanted to, a luxury we had never known.

We never intended to stay in California. Oh, we enjoyed it, so much so that we vowed to return. But soon after I had recovered from travel, we set to reading the newspapers that came in by train from Reno and from San Francisco, scanning the 'help wanted' ads, and putting out word through anyone we could find that Ike was available for hire. We clung to the hope that he could practice his profession. In that regard, this outpost of western states presented us with a double-edged sword: Although there were few Jewish communities seeking an educator, there were few Jewish educators for them to choose from: If we could identify a job, Ike was likely to be the only qualified applicant.

We were willing to relocate; indeed, we hoped to resettle in a stable community with family values, and while we were in no position to be choosy, we hoped, at least, for something more respectable than an economy fueled by motion pictures and night clubs. We wanted a family of our own, but knew we needed steady income and solid surroundings to support such an enterprise.

Weeks went by without a word, without even the hint of prospective work. Meanwhile, Ike worked odd jobs at day laborers' wages—stacking stock for a general storekeeper, unloading freight from the occasional cargo train, washing dishes at a coffee shop. Then, suddenly, with neither fanfare nor warning, opportunity knocked on our hotel room door.

*

In this enclave of starlets strutting for talent scouts, and musicians dickering with managers, one Jew could easily spot another. So it was, one night at dinner, that we noticed a Jew at a table, alone. He wore his hat indoors, at the table. He wore a traveler's attire: Black overcoat, black pants and dress shoes. His beard was cropped close, styled in a goatee. He broke bread before he began his meal, his head bowed, his lips silently mouthing the Hebrew blessing known as *hamotzi*.

Ike signaled our acknowledgment with a faint smile and a nod of his head. He mouthed, "Amen," at the end of the man's prayer.

After his meal, the man approached us.

"Hello," he said, offering Ike his hand.

"Join us for coffee?" Ike offered a chair.

The man sat.

"What brings you to this part of the country?" Ike asked, just to make polite conversation.

"I am on my way to the East," the man told us. "I am in search of an educator."

"Oh?" said Ike. He took a bite.

"I had hoped to find someone here, in Los Angeles. But I have found no one who will fill the bill. I come from Portland. A small congregation, in need of the services of a teacher, or should I say, *another* teacher, and, with luck, perhaps, a cantor."

Ike and I exchanged glances of disbelief at our good fortune, trying hard to disguise our amazement as interest, yet hardly containing our enthusiasm. It sounded too good to be true, but how could we approach the subject of candidacy?

"Another teacher?" Ike asked. "Then, you are an educator, Sir?"

"A rabbi," the man answered. "And you? What brings the two of you to Los Angeles? I could not help but notice that you are not natives."

"We've always wanted to explore the West," Ike started. "And now that we are here, we find that we really enjoy the freedoms it offers. I write music—Jewish music, in fact, though I am not an ordained cantor—and the setting provides me with inspiration. But, on the whole, Los Angeles is too show-biz for us. We won't settle here for good. In fact, we are looking for someplace to call home."

"Jewish music?" the rabbi asked. "Anything I might have heard?"

Ike hummed a few notes of a few compositions.

The rabbi nodded in recognition.

"I'm just thinking," the rabbi mused. "Ever do any teaching, Mr....I'm sorry. We haven't even exchanged names. I'm Henry Koch."

"Ike Grossman," Ike said. "And this is Amalia."

I was an afterthought, which was just as well, as the rabbi would naturally presume that we were married. Wives never merited much attention, at least not in the culture we came from.

"Well, Mr. Grossman, about the teaching," Rabbi Koch returned to the subject.

"Yes, as a matter of fact, I have taught some," Ike said modestly.

"Well, this could be a rather fortuitous meeting," the rabbi said aloud to himself. Then, to us, "What do you say I stick around a couple of days, and we'll see if we don't hit it off? You may very well have saved me a trip to New York."

*

When the offer came, it was slightly beneath him: Director of Music at a reform synagogue. Ike would tutor boys for *bar mitzvah*, direct adult and children's choirs, and play the organ at services. The salary sounded like a pittance, but Rabbi Koch assured us that the cost of living in Portland was low. On the other hand, we had no better offers. We packed up our few belongings, and after a ten-minute, civil wedding service—witnessed by strangers, performed by a judge—we boarded the train, headed north, with the rabbi, who, by now, we were calling Hank.

Our dream of a Jewish wedding ceremony on hold until Ike could obtain a Jewish divorce, we faced the future bright-eyed and full of hope. The temple helped us find a place, a pleasant apartment, affordable, as promised, within walking distance from both the synagogue and the downtown—a few square blocks of shops and pushcarts.

While Hank had been our touchstone, our first friend, the rest of the congregation welcomed us warmly, too. They especially appreciated Ike's *haimishe* way. Most of the congregants had come from the East, although a few hailed from Canada. Ike reminded them of home.

In religion school, Ike saw something special in each of their children. He never called them "the kids," or "the class," but always referred to each by name and had an individual anecdote at the end of each day for each of the parents at dismissal time. He approached his work with freshness, with energy. And he won the people's respect in return.

While Ike settled into his new position, I settled us into our new home. There wasn't much for me to unpack: We'd brought so little in our haste to move, first from New York and then from Los Angeles. Most of our furnishings we would have to buy new, or, more likely, second-hand, but still, new to us.

In sorting through even the little we brought, I found plenty of rubbish that had to go: A couple of tattered towels, well-worn underwear (mainly his), and a badly torn shirt, among it. I decided, too, that we could part with the luggage. It was beat up. Besides, we planned to stay here, so what was the point of keeping such junk? I opened each suitcase, first mine and then Ike's, to make sure I'd retrieved all the contents of each. Peeking out of a pocket inside Ike's, I found two rumpled sheets of tissue paper.

I uncrumpled them, read them, was moved to tears. I knew all along that Ike was a *mensch*; the carbon copies of his letters confirmed to me, again, that the man I loved was, indeed, a prince.

*

November 4, 1929

Dear Ruth and David,

I pray for both of you every day, pray that you are happy, that you are well, that somehow, some way, some day you will understand, and even forgive me.

Had I the abilities of a seer, or even the services of a fortune teller, I may have been able to alter my course. But I am no mystic; I am merely a man, fraught with the frailties of all mankind. My personal weakness is one for love.

Know that no love is greater than mine for you, that I will always love you, and that you have my promise, here and now, to stand by you, to stand watch, as you grow to adulthood, offering you the voice of my experience, however imperfect.

You will hear from me often, and regularly. Don't forget

Your loving,
Poppy

And this:

November 4, 1929

Dear Israel,

I know that I have shamed the family, and that, as a result, I will never again be welcome at home. For this, I have the greatest regret. I hope I have not left too much of a shambles in my wake.

It is not easy to make an island of oneself: I doubt that anyone there, save you, could understand my despair, my pain. You alone witnessed my struggle; you watched me cope—badly, at that. If only I could have fulfilled my obligation without betraying myself, without living a lie. In the end, that was what decided it.

I tried everything within my power, even leaving our home for a year, but for reasons I do not fully understand, I could not abandon my heart, even when I abandoned my love.

As it turned out, Nevada is an expeditious state: I already have obtained a civil divorce, and will see to the *get* once Amalia and I have recovered from the shake-up I have precipitated. (It has hardly been easy for her, either, to leave the only life she knew.) In the meanwhile, I entrust you, both as my collaborator and my brother, to forward all royalties from our published work to Bella and the children. It will hardly sustain them, but perhaps, at least, it will convey to them that I never intended to forsake them.

I expect no response from you, brother. Indeed, I understand, acutely, the predicament I put you in by writing you at all.

So, unless you wish to continue our correspondence, I will point myself on a new path, toward a new life, with, at last, the *right* wife, in, of all places, the wild west!

Ever your loving brother,
Isaac E. Grossman

*

About six months later, we moved again, this time to a house with Ike's name on the property deed. Hank had asked us to stay in Portland for good, and the temple president offered to make a down payment on a house to express his personal gratitude for Ike's services. With the temple as co-signator on our bank loan, we found ourselves permanently in place.

New life stirred within me, and contentment filled my heart.

ABOUT THE AUTHOR

Susan Wolfe, an award-winning author and community leader, is a graduate of Stanford University and the prestigious Wexner Heritage Foundation program in Jewish studies. Her professional honors include the Kathryn D. Hansen Publication Award for 1994. She and her family live in Palo Alto, California.

I love the
alliteration
imagination

when did choc. covered
gelt originate - what year?

Made in the USA